JUN

FRIENDS
OF ACPL

Schoolroom
ZOO

Other books by Catherine Woolley

TWO HUNDRED PENNIES

GINNIE AND GENEVA

DAVID'S RAILROAD

Schoolroom ZOO

CATHERINE WOOLLEY

illustrated by
IRIS BEATTY JOHNSON

William Morrow and Company, New York 1950

jW882a

Third Printing, July, 1954.
Copyright, 1950, by Catherine Woolley.
Printed in the United States of America.
All rights reserved.
Published simultaneously in the Dominion of Canada.

With thanks to ELISABETH
and her balsam pillow!

U. S. 981261

CONTENTS

Schoolroom
ZOO

CHAPTER 1

THE RED EFT

THE last piece of chocolate brownie disappeared into Ellie's mouth. She brushed the crumbs from her hands and got up from the rock she was sitting on. The campfire Daddy had built to toast the hot dogs was dying down. Mother stood close to it, holding out her hands to the glowing coals.

"Shall I get some more wood, Dad?" Andy asked.

"Do we need it? Aren't we going for a little hike?" Daddy replied.

"Yes!" Ellie cried eagerly.

"We'd better get moving," Mother added, with a shiver in spite of the fire, and began to gather cups and paper plates.

Mother and Daddy, eleven-year-old Andy, and Ellie, who was eight, were having their first picnic of the season this Saturday in March. There was a bite to the wind, but the spot they had found for their lunch here in the woods was sheltered by high rocks on one side. On the other side a crystal clear spring, bubbling mysteriously from the dark earth, hurried busily away over the pebbles, sparkling in the thin sunlight that filtered through the trees.

"I'm going to get another drink," Ellie said, and ran to lie flat on the ground and put her face down to the icy water. She came up, her face dripping and rosy, and scrambled to her feet. She came dancing back to the fire, brushing off

the bits of dead leaves that clung to her hands.
Mother was putting the last picnic things in one
of the knapsacks. Daddy and Andy were raking
out the embers with sticks.

"Well, let's go." Daddy shouldered the big
knapsack, Andy the smaller one. They took a
last look around their lunch spot.

Ellie skipped ahead along the forest trail. Her
braids bobbed, her arms pumped, her coat
flopped open—sure signs that Ellie was happy.
She loved to be out in the woods.

March winds howled through the bare treetops.
"Button your jacket, Ellie," Mother called.

Ellie stopped to protest. "I'm hot!" She felt
glowing inside and out, from food and the fire
and excitement and running.

"Me too." Andy hopped ahead of Ellie, leap-
ing from dry spot to dry spot in the wet, matted
leaves that lined the trail. Ellie ran after him,
breathless and eager.

"What's the rush, you two?" Daddy called from
the rear of the procession. "Let's see things as
we go along."

Ellie slowed down and looked around her at the ground. There were no flowers so early— only the ferns and skunk cabbage and other plants growing among the leaves.

Then Ellie suddenly stopped short before a scrap of bright orange in the path. She had to look close before she saw it was a tiny creature only a couple of inches long, lying motionless in the brown leaves.

"Look!" Ellie cried. "A lizard!"

Andy turned back. Mother and Daddy came up. "That's not a lizard," Daddy said. "It's a red eft."

The eft tried to scramble awkwardly away as Ellie stooped, but she picked him up. He struggled a little in her clasp, then sat on her hand warily but without resistance. He was so light that except for the tiny dry pressure of his feet and tail she could feel nothing. He crawled up her arm as Ellie reached out a finger to touch his back.

"Oh, can I keep him, Mother?" Ellie begged.

"If you want to."

"Put him in the empty fruit-juice can," Daddy suggested.

"Can't he get out?"

"He can't climb up such a smooth surface."

Mother got the empty can from the knapsack. Ellie put the eft in it. "I'm going to take him home!" she declared, peering down at him. "And"—she looked up—"what can his name be?"

"Effie the Eft," Andy suggested.

"No." Ellie scowled. What an insulting name for anything as noble sounding as a red eft! Red eft sounded like a hero, like the Black Knight or something. Ellie walked along slowly, carrying the can, her eyes on the eft. She stumbled, heedless of rocks and roots in the path.

"I know," she exclaimed. She turned to face Mother and Daddy, her eyes shining. "Rocky! His name can be Rocky."

"Rocky, the Red Eft," Mother said, smiling at her.

Mother and Andy went ahead. Ellie and Daddy walked together.

"Oh goodie, goodie! I've got an eft!" Ellie

sang softly to herself, studying Rocky. She tripped over a stone.

"You'll fall flat on your face!" Daddy warned.

The sun's rays slanted across the trees. The wind boomed in the bare branches. Ellie fumbled at the buttons of her coat with one hand.

"Here's the road," Daddy said. He pulled out his watch. "We'd better go back to the car. It'll be nearly dinnertime when we get home."

Ellie was anxious to get home now. She hurried along the road, one hand in Daddy's. "I want to fix a house for Rocky," she told him. "I'll fix a nice one and he'll like it!"

When the car stopped in front of the house, Ellie sat still, intent on gazing down at the eft in his can. Mother held the front seat tipped up.

Andy scrambled out. "Hey, will you please unlock the door, Mother, so I can get my catcher's mitt?" he said.

"Take one of the knapsacks in," Mother said. "Ellie, are you planning to stay there?"

Ellie climbed down carefully, holding the can in both hands.

"Please bring the toasting forks," Mother told her, going ahead.

"I can't." Ellie stood on the sidewalk, still looking with fascination into the can.

Andy gave her a little shove with his elbow as he went by, carrying the knapsack. "Get out of the way, El," he said good-naturedly.

Ellie hardly noticed.

The screen door banged as a shaggy shape lumbered out and came heavily down the steps. Old Pete, part collie, part St. Bernard, walked painfully because his feet hurt, but his plumy tail waved in affectionate greeting. Ellie held out the can and Pete sniffed the eft, a bit puzzled. Then he licked Ellie's hand with his warm tongue, to assure her that anything she brought home was all right with him. Andy came out with his mitt and disappeared across the street.

"Hello, Ellie."

Ellie turned and looked up. It was Lilac Hammond, who was in her class at school. Lilac was carrying a roll of music. She must be going home from her music lesson.

"Hello, Lilac," Ellie cried. "I went on a picnic and see what I found!" She paused to reach into the can for Rocky and held him out. "Look!"

Lilac gave one startled look and jumped backward. "Ugh!" she cried.

Ellie looked up at her in astonishment. "It's only a little eft!"

Lilac backed away further. "Ugh! The squirmy, ugly thing! Take it away!"

"He is not ugly!" Ellie said indignantly.

"He is!"

"He is not!"

"Yes, he is." Lilac was backing slowly.

"You stop!" Ellie cried, stamping her foot. Suddenly she dumped Rocky in the can and began to chase Lilac. "You stop calling him names or I'll—put—him—right—on you!"

Lilac gave a screech, turned, and fled down the street. Ellie chased her past the next house, then slowed down.

"And he isn't squirmy, either!" she shouted. Thoroughly indignant, she looked after Lilac for

a moment before she turned and went slowly
back. She took the eft out again and bent her
head down to the little creature. "Don't you
care, Rocky," Ellie apologized to his hurt feelings.

"Hi, Ellie!" From up the street a figure came
skating toward her. It was six-year-old Janie,
who lived next door. Janie's short golden curls
bobbed and her arms pumped wildly as she
skated.

"Hi, Janie!" Ellie yelled back. She forgot
Lilac and stood waiting for Janie. Here was
someone who would like Rocky. Janie looks
just like a baby angel, she thought, as Janie drew
nearer. So tiny, with golden ringlets, great blue
eyes, and a little pink face shaped like a heart.

The angel turned around on her skates as she
reached Ellie. Her arms flew up, her legs flew
out, and down she sat with a surprised look and
a small grunt.

"Look what I've got, Janie!" Ellie cried.

"What?" Janie reared up backward and
brushed her hands off on her skirt. "Let me
see."

Ellie held out the eft.

"Oh, the darling, darling little—what *is* it, Ellie? Did you get him at the picnic?"

Ellie nodded. "He's a red eft. His name is Rocky and I'm going to keep him for a pet."

"If he has any baby red efts, can I have one?"

"Yes."

"O.K." Satisfied, Janie skated beside Ellie. They went up Ellie's walk. Janie clumped up the steps on her skates. Mother came out of the kitchen with her apron on as Ellie pushed open the door.

"What are you going to put your eft in?" Mother asked. "Janie, take your skates off if you're coming in. Of course," Mother added, "Esther won't like your pet, you know."

Esther was Ellie's sister, almost thirteen. She did not share Ellie's interest in nature.

"But he doesn't bite," Ellie protested. "And he isn't squirmy and ugly. Lilac said he was! Anyway, I'm going to keep him in a jar with some water and a little rock in it and he can't get out, so Esther needn't be afraid."

"We'd better look for a jar," Mother said.

"Here, Janie." Ellie held out the eft. "You can hold Rocky while I look."

Janie accepted the eft and sat down on the edge of a chair in the living room. She held Rocky close to her chin and spoke tenderly to him.

"Here's a large mayonnaise jar," Mother called. "Will that do?"

Ellie went to see. "Yes! I'll put in the leaves I brought, too, so he'll feel right at home. And Daddy said I should put some water in a little jar top for his drinking fountain."

Rocky took to his new home quietly.

"I'll bet he's hungry," Janie said.

Ellie observed the little animal and frowned thoughtfully. "What does he eat, Mother?"

"Bugs, I suppose," Mother told her. "In the woods he catches live bugs."

"Come on, Janie, let's get some bugs," Ellie said.

They went out in the back yard and looked around. "There's some ants," Janie pointed out.

Ellie couldn't bear to put a live ant in Rocky's den. Neither could she bear to kill an ant or any kind of bug. Janie seemed to read her thoughts. "I could squash some," she offered. "I could squash 'em softly and scoop 'em up."

"No! Let's look some more." Ellie wandered into the yard, leaving the ants to scurry about their business.

But the right bugs for Rocky's dinner seemed hard to come by and the girls finally sat down on the back steps to eat cookies and consider. A fly buzzed around them.

"There!" Ellie exclaimed. "I don't mind if we catch that fly for Rocky."

Janie went after the sluggish fly, caught it in her hands, and they carried it in to Rocky. But Rocky didn't seem hungry. He sat there quietly, not touching the meat—strictly fresh—they set before him.

"I bet he's homesick," Ellie decided. "I'm going to put him on the rug because it's green, like the woods, and he'll like it."

They put Rocky on the rug and formed a

circle of arms and legs around him, although Rocky showed no sign of running away.

"Ellie, you can have Rocky for your pet in the pet show," Janie said.

Ellie nodded. "I know." The pet show was to be held at the playground during Easter vacation.

"I bet he'll get a prize," Janie said, hanging over Rocky.

There was a noise like an army storming the front steps. The door burst open and slammed shut, shaking the whole house like thunder. It was only Andy, panting and dirty, with his hair rumpled and his mitt in his hand. Andy threw himself down on the floor and picked Rocky up for a moment before he went on into the kitchen.

Mother began to set the dining-room table. Daddy came in from working on the car. He tousled Ellie's hair and gave Janie's curls a tweak. He stopped a moment to watch Rocky.

"He's a handsome fellow," Daddy said. "Well, old Pete'll make one bite of him."

"Pete won't eat him!" Ellie said indignantly.

Then she grinned and wrinkled her nose at Daddy. He was fooling, of course.

"Maybe he'd like to play with the mouse we've got in the kitchen," Daddy remarked as he left them.

Ellie had one ear toward the kitchen now, where the family was assembled. Good dinner smells were beginning to drift in. Ellie wanted to be out there talking over the picnic. "You'd better go home, Janie," she said. "Our supper's almost ready."

Janie's ringlets were bent over Rocky. "I don't have to go yet."

"Yes you do, Janie. You can come back tomorrow."

"O.K." Janie got obediently to her feet and departed, carrying her skates. Ellie closed the door and skipped into the kitchen.

It was ten minutes later that she remembered Rocky, left on the living-room floor. But Rocky wasn't there. Ellie looked all around before she called the family for help. He couldn't have gone very far.

They looked and looked, but there was no Rocky.

"Now if you were an eft, Andy, where would you go?" Daddy inquired.

They tried imagining they were efts. They looked in the corners, under chairs, in the cold fireplace. No Rocky. While they were hunting, Esther came home and stood watching them from the hall. "What's the matter?" she asked.

"Ellie's lost an eft," Mother explained.

"An eft? What's that?"

"A red eft, like a salamander only littler," Ellie told her. "He's very pretty, Esther, and he doesn't bite."

"Oh!" An expression of disgust crossed Esther's face. "Oh," she said again in a different tone, "it was the most wonderful party!"

"Was it, dear?" Mother glanced at the clock. "We've got to have supper," she told the family. "You'll have to find Rocky later."

At the table Esther chattered away about the party. Ellie listened with half her attention, the other half on Rocky.

"Do you think he could get outdoors?" she asked Daddy.

"Who?" Esther demanded.

"Rocky."

"Who?"

"My red eft."

"Oh!" Esther said.   "And the refreshments, Mother!   We had . . ."

"Maybe he doesn't like flies," Ellie said thoughtfully.

"Flies?"   Esther's brown eyes turned on Ellie in horror.

"Rocky, I mean."

"Oh, Ellie!   You're simply disgusting!"

"I'm not either."   Injured, Ellie looked at Mother, who smiled at her reassuringly and said, "Esther!"

"Anyway," Esther went on, "everything was just beautiful.   And I want to have a party on my birthday, Mother, and invite all the girls who were there today."

"All right, dear.   I think we can manage."

Ellie and Esther began to clear the table.   "Do

I have to dry dishes, Mother?" Ellie asked anxiously. "I want to look for Rocky."

Andy spoke up quickly. "Oh, come on, El. I'll help you dry and Es can put away. Then we can all look."

Ellie looked at him in surprise. My goodness, she thought, what's got into Andy, drying dishes?

Ellie dried the glasses. Esther moved back and forth in a happy glow. Andy wasn't being much help after all. He kept grabbing glasses from Ellie's hands and thrusting them at Esther.

"Here's the plates, Es." Andy gave them to her. He's in an awful hurry, Ellie thought, picking up some silver. She especially liked to dry silver. She liked the feeling of the smooth, hot knives and forks and spoons slipping between the clean towel and her fingers.

Andy waited for her to dry the silver. "Here, Es, here's the silver to put away." Esther took it dreamily and wandered in to the sideboard in the dining room.

Suddenly there was a bloodcurdling shriek. Ellie jumped and a pan fell out of her hand with

a bang. Mother jerked her hands from the water.
Esther came flying into the kitchen, white as a
ghost.

"What's the matter?" Mother gasped.

"O-h-h! I put my hand—right on—something
—awful!" Esther shuddered, and shook her hand
as if to shake some horrid thing off.

Ellie gazed at her, almost as terrified as Esther
herself.

"I think"—Esther shuddered again—"it's that
—thing—of Ellie's!"

Ellie suddenly came to life. "Where, Esther,
where?"

"In the—silver drawer!"

There was Rocky, lying quietly among the
oyster forks. Ellie took him out and carried him
carefully but quickly to his mayonnaise jar.

"Now, Ellie," Mother said, when Esther had
calmed down, "if you're going to keep that eft,
you keep him in the jar!"

"And don't you ever, ever let him out again,
do you hear?" Esther stormed, furious now that
she was over her fright.

"Better keep him in your room, Ellie," Daddy said.

Ellie faced her family. She had to defend Rocky. "But he can't climb out of the jar! Daddy, you said . . ." She paused. Daddy had said efts couldn't climb up a smooth surface. Then how had Rocky climbed up the sideboard and into the drawer? "But," Ellie faltered, "I don't see how . . ."

Her eyes sought her father's. Daddy was looking at Andy. Ellie's gaze traveled to her brother. Behind the backs of Mother and Esther, Andy deliberately winked.

"Well, hm-m, hm-m!" said Daddy, clearing his throat hard. "I'd better go and put the car away." And he hurried out.

Slowly understanding spread through Ellie. Andy had done it! Oh, he was awful! A giggle suddenly burst out before she clapped her hand over her mouth.

"And it isn't funny, either!" Esther said fiercely.

Ellie pressed her lips together hard. She put

both hands over her mouth. It was no use. The giggles overflowed through her fingers.

"Ellie!" Mother said.

But Ellie had caught Andy's eye again. Andy was grinning openly now and Ellie took away her hands and laughed out loud.

"You're an old silly, Es," Andy said, wandering out of the room still grinning.

"Esther's an old silly! Esther's an old silly!" Ellie echoed.

Esther looked at Mother for help, gave a gasp, and ran into the kitchen.

"Ellie, I'm ashamed of you!" Mother said sternly. "Now you stop teasing your sister. And you take that eft upstairs and keep him there or he'll disappear. Do you understand me?"

Ellie sobered down. She nodded. Tenderly she picked up Rocky in his jar and turned toward the stairs. But part way up she began to giggle again. Afraid of a darling little eft that wouldn't hurt a thing! Well, if Esther was so silly, served her right to get scared. She ought to put Rocky in Esther's bed to make her really scared.

No, Mother would take Rocky away if she did that. But Andy was funny! She must ask him whether Rocky was in the drawer while they were hunting, or whether he found him later and put him there.

"Well," she murmured into Rocky's jar, "you can stay in my room. Because I love you anyway. And Janie loves you, and Andy . . ." She hesitated, not sure whether Andy loved Rocky or just loved a joke. "Anyway," she told the eft, "we'll bring you some nice fresh bugs to eat tomorrow. And you'll like it here. Honest!"

CHAPTER 2

THE PET SHOW

IT was a few days before Easter, and Mother had met Ellie and Esther at school to go downtown and buy spring coats.

Walking from the bus to the store, Ellie skipped ahead of Mother and Esther. The sun felt warm on her bare head this afternoon. Downtown was all decked out in Easter trim-

34

mings. Candy shops displayed huge chocolate bunnies and fancy Easter eggs. Pots of blue and pink hyacinths and great white lilies overflowed florist shops, crowding the sidewalks. They sent up the smell of warm, wet earth and Ellie sniffed a strong flower fragrance as she passed.

"Easter's coming! Easter's coming!" she sang to herself, skipping along.

A crowd had gathered in front of a shop window. Ellie paused. "I want to see!" she said to Mother. She stood on tiptoe. She stooped down. Finally she ducked under a woman's arm, squeezed between two boys, ducked and squeezed again, and arrived in front of the window.

"Oh!" Ellie breathed.

There were two sections to the window. One was filled with baby chicks—tiny, fluffy, peeping chicks. The other half held rabbits—big, soft, white bunny rabbits with quivering noses and long, pink-lined ears.

Ellie stood entranced. She forgot where she was. She forgot everything until she heard Mother's and Esther's voices behind her.

"Oh!" Ellie begged, clasping her hands but not taking her eyes from the rabbits. "Can I have a bunny rabbit, Mother? Can I, please? Or can I just have a baby chicken?"

"Oh, darling." Mother put an arm around her. "Not now, dear."

"No, Ellie, you can't!" Esther said.

"Oh, please, please, Mother!" Ellie moaned, ignoring Esther.

Mother laughed a little and reached for Ellie's hand. "We already have Pete and Rocky—and a mouse!"

Ellie let herself be drawn along, making small sounds of grief and despair. How could she live without a white bunny rabbit!

But she forgot the rabbits and chicks, at least for the moment, in the excitement of buying a new coat. How cool and loose and pleasant the spring coats felt after her heavy winter one!

"Try this one," Mother said to the salesgirl. Ellie held out her arms.

"Do you like it?" Mother asked.

Ellie put her hands in the pockets and nodded.

Mother laughed. "You like them all, don't you?"

Yes, she did. Ellie thought every coat they tried on her was the one she wanted. Finally they decided on a green coat—a pretty, light green that had bits of blue and yellow and even purple in it. For Esther Mother bought a blue coat.

Mother also bought Ellie a pair of brown kid gloves, the first she had ever owned. They were beautiful shiny gloves. They had a delicious fresh leathery smell. Ellie kept poking her nose inside the paper bag and taking long sniffs that made her mouth water. Mm! What a good juicy taste those gloves would have, she thought.

Then, in no time, it was Easter. On Easter Sunday Ellie was downstairs early in her pajamas to hunt behind doors and furniture for colored eggs and chocolate rabbits and baskets full of green or purple grass in which yellow marshmallow chickens sat on jelly beans. By breakfast time there was a circle of black around her mouth from the licorice beans, and Ellie hadn't too much appetite for scrambled eggs.

After breakfast it was exciting to put on her new hat and green coat for Sunday school.

"Isn't it too cold for spring clothes?" Daddy asked, watching from behind his paper.

Ellie looked up in alarm from the gloves Mother was smoothing on her stiffly spread-out fingers. "Oh no, Daddy!" she told him anxiously. "It's *very* warm. Isn't it, Mother?"

Mother smiled into her eyes. "Of course it is!" Mother said. "With a new Easter coat? Of course it's warm!"

All Easter vacation Ellie looked forward to the pet show to be held on Friday. The little playground in the park had been opened for vacation and the pet show had been announced in school.

"I bet Rocky will win a prize," she saïd happily one morning as she and Esther were having a late breakfast.

"That horrid little thing!" Esther said in disgust.

Ellie set her lips tight and glared at her sister. She looked around to see if Mother was within hearing distance. "Better look out or I'll get Rocky and chase you with him," Ellie murmured in a low voice, a wicked eye on Esther.

Esther threw down her napkin and marched away from the table. Ellie reached over, took the piece of pecan roll left on her sister's plate, and munched it with satisfaction.

"I wish I had a pet for the pet show," Janie mourned as they admired Rocky later that morning.

"Well, I wish you had, Janie," Ellie sympathized, tapping the glass jar lightly to attract Rocky's attention.

Before the day of the pet show a pet was miraculously provided for Janie in the person of a scrawny, bedraggled cat that began to haunt her front steps. Janie's mother did not like stray cats. "Now mister, you just go away!" Ellie heard her say, shooing the cat off the back steps. But when Janie's mother went in, the cat came right back and sat patiently on the steps again.

Ellie and Janie were starting off for the pet show Friday, Ellie carrying Rocky's jar, Janie empty-handed, when Ellie had an idea. "I know, Janie!" she exclaimed. "Why don't you take the cat to the pet show?"

Janie stood still. "I will!" she decided. She ran up to the cat on the front steps of her house and was lugging him down the walk when her mother came to the door.

"Where are you going with the cat, Janie?" her mother called.

Janie turned. "I'm going to take him to the pet show."

"Oh." Janie's mother considered. "That's not a bad idea," she said. "Don't bother to bring him back. I'm sure you can find some child who'd appreciate him more than we do."

"O.K.," Janie said.

Ellie thought about that as they walked along. She was not sure anyone would want such a homely, matted-looking animal. Poor cat!

"What's his name?" she asked.

Janie frowned. "Mister," she said finally.

"Oh. Hello, Mister." Ellie patted the cat's nose.

Quite a crowd of children had gathered at the playground. Most of them carried or led a pet.

"Hi, Ellie!" It was Mary Anne, from Ellie's class.

"Hi, Mary Anne." Ellie's eyes rested on the puppy Mary Anne held on a leash. "Is that your dog?"

Mary Anne nodded. "His name's Clown."

The puppy did look like a clown. He had floppy ears, one black and one white. He cocked his head on one side and thumped his short tail cheerfully at Ellie.

"He can do tricks," Mary Anne said.

"Make him do some."

Mary Anne shook her head. "Wait till the pet show starts."

Another girl in Ellie's class arrived, carrying a kitten.

"Oh!" Ellie cried. "Let me hold him, Phyllis."

She set Rocky's jar down and Phyllis put the soft little baby cat in Ellie's arms. The kitten was gray and white and looked up at Ellie with

blue eyes in a pansy-shaped face. She cuddled
the small fur bundle against her cheek. If she
could just have a kitten! Reluctantly Ellie
handed him back. She looked around for Janie.

"Janie," Ellie said, "I don't think you ought
to expect Mister to win a prize."

"Why?" Janie said.

"Because he isn't as pretty as Phyllis's kitten."

"But he's bigger," Janie argued.

"I don't think that counts, Janie."

Ellie was not even sure now that Rocky would
win a prize. All sorts of pets were gathered in
the park—dogs, cats, a rabbit, turtles, a baby
chick, fish, a duck, even a spider.

"Come, children," the playground supervisor
called. "Line up. We're going to begin the
judging."

The judges were a man and two ladies. As
the children filed past with their pets, the judges
looked each one over and jotted down notes on
a pad of paper.

Mary Anne's Clown did his tricks for the
judges. He chased his tail, danced, rolled over,

and said his prayers. Phyllis put her kitten down and he fluffed up his fur and danced sidewise with his tail sticking straight up.

Ellie wished Rocky had some tricks. As a last-minute thought she took him out of the jar and put him on her arm as she neared the judges. Rocky sat there quietly.

When the last pet had been shown, the judges went off by themselves and talked and compared notes. Then the supervisor called the children together again. They stood in an expectant circle, holding their pets.

"Here is the decision of the judges," she said. "First prize goes to Clown, the puppy."

The children clapped their hands while Clown frisked and barked as if he understood the whole thing. Smiling proudly, Mary Anne went up to receive the game of ring toss which was the first prize.

"Second prize," the supervisor said, "goes to this little blue-eyed kitten." Phyllis received a game for her prize, too.

"There are only two prizes," the supervisor

said, "but the judges feel that Rocky, the red eft, should have third place in the show. So they have given him honorable mention."

She smiled at Ellie, who stood holding Rocky and looking at her anxiously. "I'm sorry that there is no prize for Rocky, Ellie," the supervisor said.

Suddenly Janie, standing beside Ellie, put up her hand. That made her drop Mister.

"Yes?" the supervisor said.

Janie was busy collecting Mister again and couldn't speak for a minute. Finally she straightened up, pushing Mister up in her arms with one knee. "I know what Ellie could have for her prize," she said.

"What could she have?"

"She could have Mister."

"Mister?"

"Here he is." Janie held Mister out.

"Oh!" The supervisor looked doubtful. "But you don't want to give your cat away!"

"Yes I do," Janie explained. "He isn't our cat. He only visits on our front steps. My

mother said for me not to bother to bring him back. She said for me to find some child who would appreciate him more than us."

"Oh, I see." The supervisor turned to Ellie. "Well, Ellie, would you like Mister for the third prize?"

Ellie thought it over. She looked at Mister. He certainly wasn't much like Phyllis's kitten. She'd rather have that soft, cute little kitten.

But Mister was a poor cat without any home. Ellie remembered how patiently and lonesomely he sat on Janie's steps. And probably nobody else would want him.

"I better take him," she told the supervisor, "because he needs a kind home."

Janie carried Mister again on the way home, since Ellie had Rocky. They walked into Ellie's house and Janie dumped Mister on the hall floor. "I have to go now," Janie said and departed, skipping.

Mother looked up from the chair in the living room and laid down the stocking she was darning. "Is that the stray cat that's been hanging

around Janie's? Why bring him in here?"
Mother inquired.

"I won him," Ellie explained.

"Won him!"

Ellie nodded. "Yes, because Rocky was the
third-best pet, only there wasn't any third-best
prize. So Janie said Mister could be the third-
best prize because her mother doesn't appreciate
him. So he was."

"Oh my heavens!" Mother said.

She looked at Mister. Mister sat himself down
and looked at Mother. "Me-ow!" said Mister in
a faint voice, as if he hoped against hope he
might be welcome here.

"Well," Mother said finally, "he looks as if he
hasn't had a square meal in days. If we've got
a prize cat in the family, Ellie, I think you'd better feed him!"

CHAPTER 3

MISTER AND THE MOUSE

"But listen, El," Andy said, "did you have to bring home a ratty old stray cat like that?"

They were having dinner. Mister had had some dinner too, and was catching up on his sleep in a cardboard carton in the kitchen.

"Yes," Esther put in, "if we have to have a

49

cat, why can't we have a cute white Persian kitten with blue eyes?"

Ellie sighed and laid down her fork. She
shook her head at her sister. "Esther," Ellie said
patiently, "I've told you hundreds of times—
well, twelve times—I did not just choose Mister.
He just naturally *came,* on account of me having
the third-best pet. I couldn't help it if Rocky
was the third-best pet, could I? And when a cat
just naturally *comes* to you, you have to take
him! Don't you, Mother?"

Mother gave a sigh, too. "I suppose so, dear."

"Nuts," said Andy.

"Well, if he stays he'd better catch that mouse,"
Daddy commented, piling more mashed potato
on Andy's plate.

"Hey, Dad, that's a good idea," Andy said. "If
he catches the mouse he can stay!"

Ellie looked from her father to her brother in
dismay. She had caught a glimpse of the mouse
once when it scurried across the kitchen floor and
disappeared. Such a little mouse to set a big
cat on. Oh dear!

"Let him stay in the kitchen tonight," Daddy said, "and see what happens."

They hadn't seriously tried to catch the mouse; they had only talked about setting the trap some time. Ellie thought hard as she helped clear the table.

"Andy," she said when the dishes were done, "will you please get the mousetrap for me?"

He wrinkled his face into a question mark. "What for, for gosh sake?"

"I just want it. Please, please! I won't set it or anything."

Andy shook his head as if she were hopeless. "I don't get the idea. What good is a mousetrap if you don't set it? Some people are screwy."

Nevertheless he brought the trap from the cellar. "O.K.," he said, "but don't catch your finger now."

"I won't."

Ellie took the trap gingerly and looked around the kitchen. Under the table would be the best place. If she put it there, but didn't set it, the mouse would see it and say to himself, "Ha! A trap! These people want to catch me." And he'd run away and never come back.

That, at least, was what Ellie, putting the trap in plain sight as a warning, hoped the mouse would say to himself.

But she wasn't trusting entirely to the trap. She went up to her room, took her blue bag from the drawer, and extracted a quarter—her week's allowance paid that day—and a couple of dimes and some pennies left over from other weeks. Then she slipped quietly out the back door.

Down on Main Avenue the stores were open Friday night. Ellie hurried, so she would not be missed at home. In the supermarket she hunted until she found the canned fish, looked the cans and their prices over carefully, and bought three tins of mackerel. That was cheap and, she hoped, filling. She paid for the cans and took them home, once more slipping through the back door.

Fortunately Mother had gone next door to talk to Janie's mother. Daddy and Esther and Andy were playing rummy, and the radio was blaring loudly enough to drown out Ellie's move-ments. They thought she was up in her room.

Ellie got out the can opener while Mister sat and watched her. The top was only half off, and Ellie's nose was beginning to wrinkle in distaste at the oily, fishy odor when Mister showed signs of active interest.

"Me-ow!" said Mister, rubbing and twisting against Ellie's legs.

There was no problem in getting him to follow her up the back stairs. In her room she dumped the fish into a saucer and watched Mister eat.

He ate it all, though the last few bites called for almost more effort than Mister, still feeling the effects of a large dinner, was able to put forth. He struggled through the last mouthful, then sat back looking a trifle sick and licked his chops.

Ellie gave a sigh of relief. Now, surely, the mouse was safe for one night at least. Mister would have no interest in a tasty snack of mouse before morning.

Mother noticed the trap when she came home. "Who put the trap here?" she called.

Ellie flew up from the rummy game. "I did! Leave it there!"

"But, honey, it isn't set."

"I don't want it set! I don't want it set!" Ellie protested. "I just want the mouse to see it, so he'll go away."

They all looked at her. Andy and Esther shouted with laughter, while Daddy shook a little behind his pipe. Ellie went and hid her head in Mother's lap.

She was glad they didn't know about the empty mackerel can and the two unopened ones in the back of her closet.

Mister did not catch the mouse that night. The next two nights Ellie fed him the rest of the mackerel. Daddy remarked it was amazing how that cat had plumped up in two days, though he didn't seem to be a mouser. Mother said she couldn't understand why she kept smelling fish. Ellie poked three empty mackerel cans down in the garbage, with Mister tight at her heels blissfully sniffing mackerel on the air.

But now Ellie's allowance was gone, and she

would not have any more money until Friday.

Some time during the next night Ellie woke up suddenly, sure that Mister, in the kitchen, was about to catch the mouse. At the foot of her bed where Pete slept, though it was much too narrow to be really comfortable for him, the old dog raised his head.

Ellie couldn't stand it. She slipped out of bed, tiptoed into the quiet hall where the night light was burning, closed her door softly to prevent Pete from following, and felt her way down the carpeted stairs.

When she snapped on the light in the kitchen, Mister looked up, sat up, yawned, and watched to see if Ellie would open a can of mackerel. But Ellie only sat down on a chair to watch for the mouse and protect him from a hungry Mister.

Mister yawned again, curled up on his blankets, and went to sleep.

Ellie waited. It was very still, so still the silence began to beat against her eardrums like noise. Her eyelids drooped. She swayed back and forth a little on the chair.

Ellie slept. Mister slept. And the mouse crept out of his tiny hole and scurried across the floor toward Ellie, his quivery nose and little whiskered face uplifted.

Ellie started suddenly. Her eyes opened and she saw the mouse. She and the mouse stared at one another. Then the mouse ran across the floor like a shadow and disappeared. Mister sat up, looking grumpy.

Oh dear, Ellie thought, how sleepy I am! I can't stay here one minute longer!

She stumbled upstairs and was asleep before her head touched the pillow. In the morning Ellie wasn't quite sure whether she had made that midnight visit to the kitchen or dreamed it. She lay in bed a few minutes, thinking about the little mouse with the whiskers and the quivering nose. An idea began to form in her mind.

If she could catch the mouse herself, and make a pet of it, and keep it in a nice big box with holes in it, the mouse would be safe from Mister. As for Mister, surely the family wouldn't really make her get rid of him.

Ellie made her plans carefully. After school she went down to the basement and looked over the old boxes Mother saved. Here was a cigar box. Ellie sniffed. The wood held the strong, stale smell of tobacco. Would a little mouse like that? A chocolaty smell, sweet and pleasant, lingered in an old candy box. That was better, but maybe not for a mouse.

Here was just the thing! A big square tin box with a faint sugary odor of cookies clinging to it. That was right, Ellie was sure, for catching the mouse. When she had caught him, she would fix another, bigger box for him to live in.

She carried the box up to her room and punched some breathing holes in the top with the can opener. Now, with a piece of cheese extracted from the refrigerator when no one was around, she was ready. All she had to do was be sure and wake up in the night.

Ellie did wake up, with a start. Again she got out of bed, with Pete watching uneasily, took the box and cheese, and crept downstairs. Mister stretched and yawned in welcome.

She drew the chair into the middle of the room, then paused. No, she'd better sit on the floor, where she could reach the box quickly and clap the cover right on when the mouse got in it. She sat down cross-legged, laid the box on its side, and put the cheese in the box. Mister came over and smelled the cheese, but Ellie tapped his nose softly and he went back to bed. Then Ellie waited, holding the box cover, for the mouse to come.

The silence rose and whistled in her ears. She shut her eyes and swayed slightly. Mister woke to bite a flea fiercely, sighed, and slept again.

Ellie's eyes opened slowly, silently. The mouse was there, wiggling his nose at her. She sat still as a statue. The mouse scampered closer and stopped again. Now his nose was pointing at the cheese. His whiskers fairly trembled with eagerness. Oh, what a tiny mouse he is, Ellie thought. He must be a baby.

The baby mouse ventured nearer. Without a sound Mister sat up and regarded him. The mouse was thinking it over. He didn't see Mister

or the intent gleam in Mister's green eyes. Ellie's heart began to pound. Hurry up, hurry up, mouse! Get in the box!

Now the mouse seemed to take courage. He crept closer, sniffing the box with its delicious smells. Slowly, cautiously, the mouse stole up to the box.

Mister, still soundless, began to wag his rear end, ready for a swift pounce. The mouse moved. Ellie's hand tightened on the cover.

The mouse was in the box! Ellie's hand moved slowly, then swiftly. She clapped the cover over the box with a bang as Mister sprang at it. There was a brief scramble inside, then all was quiet. Mister was left to sniff in baffled bewilderment.

Ellie drew a deep breath and sat clutching the box. When she got up, her legs felt funny and shaky. But the mouse was safe!

"No!" Ellie told Mister, leaning down to flap her hand at him. "You behave!"

Her heart still beating hard with excitement, Ellie clung to the box. She snapped out the light after one last glance at Mister, who regarded her with injured innocence.

Back in her room, just to be sure, Ellie fastened the box shut with a large rubber band borrowed for the purpose. Pete greeted her with obvious relief, wagging his tail, but he sniffed with suspicion at the boxed mouse.

"Ellie, what's the matter?" Mother's voice called sleepily.

Ellie jumped, put the box on her dresser, and turned out the light. "Nothing," she called back softly, scrambling under the covers. "I was just —up."

The mattress sagged as Pete boosted himself up and stretched out across the bed again with a deep sigh. Ellie pushed her cold toes under his warm body and cuddled deeper into the blankets.

Now, she thought happily, Mister can't get him! It's lucky I went down, because he never saw the trap. Tomorrow I'll fix a real house for the mouse. A house for the mouse. A house— a house . . .

Ellie was asleep.

CHAPTER 4

ESTHER HAS A BIRTHDAY PARTY

MISTER stayed on, accepted by Andy and Esther as his coat grew shiny and his sleek sides rippled under the satiny fur. The mouse was not accepted, but stayed anyway. Esther fumed at Ellie for having a mouse and wouldn't go near Ellie's room. Ellie was not allowed to bring the mouse out, ever.

The mouse was still in his cookie box, equipped now with drinking water and crumpled paper. Daddy said he would try to fix a better house for him if Ellie insisted on keeping him. Andy said he would, too. But nobody got around to doing it. The cracker box was good and big, however, so Ellie didn't worry too much.

Every day she built four walls with her old blocks and let Mouse run about inside them. By hovering over the fort, she kept him there. Losing fear of his tin box, Mouse learned to go back in when she put down food.

As for relations between Mister and Mouse, Ellie felt the two had come to be, if not near and dear friends, at least mutually recognized members of the household. She often let Mister look at Mouse as he wandered about his run. She explained to the cat that Mouse had as much right there as he had.

Mister seemed to get the idea. He always relaxed after a while and settled down to watch Mouse with fascinated but apparently harmless interest.

Whether Mouse felt as kindly toward Mister, Ellie wasn't sure. But after the big whiskered face had gazed down upon the little whiskered face a number of times and nothing had come of it, Mouse stopped his frantic scurrying at sight of Mister and paid no attention.

Sometimes Pete lumbered up to Ellie's room and looked on. Pete never barked at Mister, but sometimes he made a gruff remark or two at the mouse, as if so much scuttling about made him nervous.

Every day, too, Ellie took Rocky for a walk in the garden, watching him closely lest he wander too far.

For some time now the whole household—at least Ellie, Esther, and Mother—had been looking forward to Esther's birthday party. It was to be a six-o'clock supper. Andy and Daddy were banished for the day. They were planning to enjoy hot dogs together at a diner downtown.

There was a discussion one morning at breakfast as to whether Ellie was to eat at the party table.

"Ellie wiggles so," Esther said. "And she tips things over."

Ellie began to feel all pushed down and sick inside from disappointment.

Then Esther looked at her and said, "Well, I guess you can, Ellie."

Ellie clapped her hands and tipped over her glass of milk.

"That's what I mean!" Esther said with a loud sigh. But Ellie was to eat at the table.

On the afternoon of the party Ellie, her cheeks flushed and her eyes shining, was even more excited, if that was possible, than Esther herself. She was all dressed up in her best plaid skirt and white ruffled blouse, with her gold chain and locket. Her braids were tied with green ribbons.

"Oh, Ellie!" Esther said, throwing her arms around her. "You look so darling!"

Esther was dressed up too, in a new salmon-colored sweater. Ellie admired her sister, with her golden-brown eyes, pale-caramel skin, and heavy fair hair that crinkled around the edges.

"So do you!" Ellie hugged her back joyfully. Esther was so often cross or impatient with her, it was wonderful now to be approved. She was going to be good and helpful all day and not let anything happen that would displease Esther on her birthday.

Ellie wandered from room to room, admiring each one. In the living room were vases of golden acacia, like sunshine. The centerpiece for the party table was an arrangement of spring flowers: tulips, jonquils, daisies, iris. Tall yellow candles rose from four silver candlesticks. It was the most beautiful table Ellie had ever seen. She walked all around it, admiring the pretty place cards and the yellow snappers that had hats inside. She found her own place card and studied it with great satisfaction.

She went on into the kitchen where Mrs. Keeley, who always came to help with parties, was cutting up cooked chicken into a big kettle. Mother was stuffing stalks of celery with cheese.

Mm! Ellie's mouth watered. They were going to have potato chips too, and tomato jelly with chopped things in it. And ice cream, of course, and a birthday cake with candles! Ellie tiptoed to the closet to peek at the cake on the shelf. It had a beautiful creamy orange icing, Esther's favorite, and yellow candles ready to light.

The cream cheese reminded her of Mouse. He hadn't had his exercise today. Before the party began, Ellie decided, she would go up and let him out for a while.

Ellie casually scooped a bit of cream cheese from a piece of celery when Mother's back was turned, and carried it upstairs on her stuck-out first finger. There she transferred it to a bit of paper torn from a magazine.

She dragged the box of blocks from a corner, kneeled down, and began to set up the walls necessary for Mouse's daily run. She did not build them as high as usual, because there wasn't much time before the guests were due to arrive. Then she let Mouse out of his box and put the cream cheese down inside the fort.

Pete wandered in and, shortly after, Mister.

Pete had been sniffing around the decorated table and knew something was going on, so he thought it wise to keep an eye on the family. Mister was just afraid he might miss something.

"Now you both be good," Ellie warned them, as she always did. "This little tiny mouse won't hurt you and don't you hurt him!" Still kneeling on the floor, she supervised Mouse's play time.

She glanced up at Rocky in his mayonnaise jar. Poor Rocky hadn't had his walk today, either. I'd better let him out right here for some exercise, Ellie thought.

Pete wouldn't touch Rocky, she knew, and Mister was used to him, because Mister often went with Rocky and Ellie on their daily stroll in the garden. Mister liked Rocky's bright color and sometimes put out his paw gently as if he would like to play with him.

So Ellie put Rocky on the floor, and Mister transferred his interest from Mouse to Rocky and sniffed. Then Mister tucked his paws in neatly and settled down to watch the eft.

Downstairs the doorbell rang. Oh, the party was beginning! Ellie started to scramble to her feet, then hesitated, casting a doubtful look at the animals. Rocky and Mouse had hardly been out a minute; surely they'd be all right if she just shut the door and left them.

"You be good," she told them. "I'll be back in a couple of minutes." She jumped up, not noticing in her haste that she had knocked down part of Mouse's wall. Closing the door, she flew downstairs as the bell rang again and the second batch of girls arrived.

Ellie's job was to show the guests up to Esther's room to leave their coats. She did this most politely, waiting to conduct them downstairs again. Then she stood in the background, happy and pleased, while Mother and Esther welcomed the guests.

Oh, how exciting it was to have a party, she thought! How pretty Esther and Mother were and how shining the house looked, all cleaned and polished, with the late sun streaming through the living-room windows. Esther's presents were heaped up on the hall table, beautiful and mysterious and promising wonderful surprises beneath their gay wrappings and ribbons.

Best of all, how good that creamed chicken smelled! Ellie thought of the orange cake and her mouth watered. She could hardly wait for supper to begin. She glanced at the clock. It was ten minutes to six now. Only ten minutes and they would file into the dining room. The candlelight would shine softly on the gleaming china and sparkling glasses. Everyone would find their places, and then the party would really begin!

The last two guests had come now. Ellie escorted them upstairs.

"I'd like to wash my hands," one of the girls said.

"Well, you can," Ellie assured her, "because we put some clean towels in the bathroom. It's right there." She waved her hand in its general direction. "I'll go down," she added. She didn't intend to miss seeing Esther open her presents.

Ellie flew down the stairs. The girls were

drifting into the living room. Esther had all the gift packages in her arms. Ellie, eyeing them, was dimly conscious of hearing Pete bark.

From upstairs came a sudden shriek. Two shrieks! Yell after yell in high-pitched, terrified voices! Down the stairs, practically falling in their haste, still screaming at the top of their lungs and tumbling over each other, came the last two guests.

Ellie felt her knees grow weak with fright. Esther stood holding the presents, frozen with horror. All the girls ran into the hall. Mother came rushing from the kitchen, her face white. Both girls clutched Mother, held on to her, babbling, their faces pale and frightened.

From upstairs, over the fracas, sounded Pete's distressed barking.

"What happened?" Mother gasped.

"What's the matter?" Esther echoed.

"Oh!" One of the girls gulped and clung closer to Mother. "We—opened—a door! We thought it was the—bathroom! And the room was full of—of—wild *animals!*"

"O-h-h!" Esther let out a deep breath and turned to Ellie. Ellie suddenly clapped her hands over her mouth in horror. She had forgotten Mouse and Rocky—and Mister and Pete!

"Oh, thank heaven!" Mother said, letting go of the girls. "I thought—I don't know what I thought!"

"But what—what kind of animals?" The guests clustered around the two frightened girls, casting nervous glances up the stairs.

"It's all right," Esther told them. "They're just Ellie's animals, loose *as usual*." She turned fiercely on her sister. Ellie shrank back.

"Go upstairs, Ellie," Mother said sternly, "and don't come down until you've caught those animals and put them away. I should certainly have thought, at a time like this . . ."

"Oh, I'm so *sorry!*" Esther apologized to her guests. "You just don't *know* what a trial it is . . ."

Ellie turned slowly to climb the stairs. All the joy had gone out of the party. The worst of it was she knew she had done wrong to leave

Rocky and Mouse out of their homes. Though how anyone could act so silly just because they saw a little mouse and a tiny eft!

But she had meant this to be a perfect day, so happy for Esther and for her, too. Now she had spoiled everything.

Pete greeted her at the door, anxious to get out and investigate the excitement. Mister lay in the middle of the floor, scarcely able to tear his eyes from Mouse, who had gotten out of his fort and, in a little lump, crouched, facing him. Rocky had backed up under a chair as far away as he could get.

They weren't doing anything, Ellie thought. All that fuss!

Her eyes fell on the little clock on her desk and her heart gave a dismal flop. Six o'clock. Time for supper. And she had to catch Mouse before she could go down.

She tiptoed to the door and listened. A babble of voices drifted up. She couldn't tell whether they were going into the dining room or not.

Ellie put Rocky in his jar and shut Mister out

in the hall. Then she got Mouse's box and sat down with it. He hadn't eaten his cream cheese. Maybe he didn't like it, and that was all she had up here. She put the cream cheese in the tipped-up box anyway and stayed there, sitting quietly beside it.

Mouse's freedom appeared to have gone to his head. He sat still, sniffing for a long time. Then he scurried off away from her. Now he was under the bed.

Oh dear! Ellie glanced frantically at the clock. She moved the box over to the bed and hitched herself along.

A faint rustle sounded in the corner. Mouse was near the clothes closet. Fortunately its door was closed. Ellie turned and faced Mouse again with the box.

Mouse was having a wonderful time exploring the room. Suppose he got out under the hall door? Ellie scrambled up as quietly as she could, grabbed the blanket from the foot of her bed and covered the crack under the door.

She sat down again. Five minutes after six.

Oh *dear!* "Come, Mouse, please! *Please,* Mouse!" Ellie begged softly and desperately.

Mouse had other ideas. Clearly he did not care for cream cheese or tin boxes. He busied himself in the shadows around the edge of the room.

A quarter past six. They were eating. A loud clatter of voices drifted up, but girls could eat and chatter at the same time. A hot tear rolled down Ellie's cheek. How *did* you catch a mouse if he wouldn't come to his box? She rubbed the tears away with the backs of her hands, then shut her eyes as more tears came up, stinging, and slid beneath her closed lids. A small sob shook Ellie. The beautiful, beautiful party! And she was missing it.

She opened her eyes. Mouse was sitting not far away, looking at her. He crept closer, sniffing the box. He was almost inside! Ellie held her breath.

Mouse turned and scuttled away. Ellie's heart sank to the pit of her stomach.

Twenty-five minutes past six. She could hear

merriment in full swing downstairs. All the exciting presents were out of their wrappers now. Supper was all eaten, birthday candles wished on and blown out, snappers snapped. Ellie felt too desolate even to cry.

Mouse was coming back. His nose quivered at sight of Ellie and his box. He came closer. Ellie did not move, but she was afraid her loudly thumping heart would scare him off.

Mouse crept cautiously forward, sniffing the cream cheese. He paused on the threshold of the box—then moved inside. Quick as a flash Ellie's hand banged on the cover, just as Esther's voice sounded and the door pushed open a crack.

"Ellie!" Esther's voice said. "Aren't you ever coming? We've waited supper half an hour!"

Ellie turned up wet, unbelieving eyes. "You *waited?*"

"Of course. Now come on!" Esther ran downstairs.

"Oh, I'm coming!" Ellie scrambled to her feet in frantic haste, pushed Mouse's cover securely in place, and fairly flew down the stairs.

"At last!" Esther said. "Now I'll open the presents and then we can have supper."

Ellie peeked around into the dining room. There stood the table, beautiful and untouched, gleaming in the tall, flickering glow of the yellow candles.

She drew a deep, quivery breath of joy. She hadn't missed the party after all!

CHAPTER 5

NO MORE PETS

THE next morning, however, in
the cold light of day and with the party glow
nearly worn off, Esther's indignation returned.
They were at Sunday breakfast in the sunny
dining room. Mother was pouring waffle batter
into the iron and a pleasant fragrance of sausages
and baking waffles filled the air.

"She nearly *ruined* my party!" Esther declared to Daddy. "I don't think she should be *allowed* to have her old animals all over the house!"

"They weren't!" Ellie said.

"Well, when people open a door by mistake, and see a roomful of—of—mice—and—*reptiles* . . ."

"Rocky is not a reptile!"

"He is too."

Ellie looked at her mother and father for help. But Mother was taking a crisp golden waffle from the iron. Daddy was busy with the last of the waffle on his plate.

"Is Rocky a reptile, Andy?" Ellie demanded.

"Yeah, I guess so."

She was too crushed to reply at once. She felt forlorn and forsaken by her family.

"Daddy, make her get rid of them!" Esther said.

Daddy took a swallow of coffee and cleared his throat. "Ellie," he said, "a mouse isn't a very good house pet."

"I keep him right in my room!" She was beginning to feel tearful.

"But your mouse hasn't the right kind of living quarters. Don't you think it's a bit hard on the mouse to keep him in a box?"

"It's a big box. And I let him out every day," Ellie answered.

"But that's hard on Es," Andy put in, grinning.

"You see, dear," Mother said, "it's a question of being considerate of other people. It makes Esther uncomfortable to have these little animals around, and yesterday they did frighten the girls terribly. After all, it's Esther's home."

"It's my home too," Ellie said. "And I like them!"

They all thought that over. Then Esther said, "Well, I don't mind your keeping Rocky so much, if you'll get rid of that awful mouse."

"That's fair enough," Andy commented.

"Besides," Daddy added, "Rocky is probably happy in captivity, and I doubt if your mouse is —especially with a cat around."

Ellie had to admit Esther's offer was reasonable. "All right," she said in a subdued tone, her eyes on her plate. "I'll get rid of Mouse."

"What are you going to do with him?" Andy inquired.

"I don't know yet."

"And you're not," Esther said firmly, "to get any other animals to run around this house and scare people out of their wits."

Ellie stared at her sister in dismay. "Not *any* kind of animals?"

"No!"

Ellie looked piteously at her mother. "I did want a white bunny rabbit some time."

"Oh, Ellie dear," Mother said, "we have no place to keep a rabbit."

"Then I wish I could have a little chicken or a baby duck."

"Little chickens and ducks turn into big chickens and ducks. The Board of Health wouldn't let you," Daddy reminded her.

Ellie reviewed the situation solemnly. "Then I can't ever, forever, have any animals except Mister and Pete and Rocky?"

Mother leaned over and squeezed her hand. "Forever's a long time, darling. And how many

little girls do you think have a cat and a dog and
a red eft?"

But Ellie felt there was not much left to live
for.

She was dressed for Sunday school. Usually
she went with Esther and Andy. But today, after
she had put on her green coat and white straw
hat and made sure her collection money was in
the blue bag, she took Mouse's box and went
next door to Janie's.

Janie was on the steps, also ready for Sunday
school, in her pink Easter coat and hat.
"What've you got Mouse's box for?" she inquired.

"Because," Ellie said, "I have to get rid of
him. Would your family like you to have Mouse
for a pet, Janie?"

"I don't know. I'll go ask." Janie disappeared into the house. She returned promptly.
"My mommie says a thousand times no thank
you," she reported.

"Oh," Ellie said. "Well, maybe someone in
Sunday school would like him. Come on, Janie,
if you're ready."

She parked Mouse's box in the coatroom at Sunday school.

The golden text this morning was "And as ye would that men should do to you, do ye also to them likewise. Luke 6:31." Ellie considered it and decided this was a good time to bring up the subject of Mouse.

"You should do to *animals* likewise, too, shouldn't you?" she asked Miss Taylor.

"Yes. Animals are God's children, just as boys and girls are," Miss Taylor answered her.

"If there's anybody in this class who would like a little mouse to do likewise to," Ellie announced, "I have a very nice one and I'll give it to them."

"Why, Ellie!" Miss Taylor said. "Is it a white mouse?"

Ellie shook her head. "Gray. Do you want to see him?"

Miss Taylor looked alarmed. "Oh no, thank you just the same. Er—where is the mouse?"

"In the coatroom."

"The coatroom!" Miss Taylor started to stand

up, then controlled herself. "He isn't—Ellie, he isn't loose, is he?"

The girls in the class squealed and the boys giggled.

Assured that Mouse was not running around the floor of the coatroom and about to invade the Sunday school, Miss Taylor got back to the lesson, or tried to. Joey Curtis began to pretend his fingers were mice running over the floor, up the chairs, and up the girls' backs. Soon, since there were six boys in the class, there were twelve finger-mice running around.

Mary Anne drew her feet up off the floor and shook the mice off her back, giving little shrieks. Ellie giggled and pushed the mice away. Joey's and George's mice met and began a scuffle. Mr. Forbes, the superintendent, came to see what the excitement was about. Ellie's class had never had so much fun before.

But no one offered to take Mouse for a pet. Ellie collected the box when Sunday school was dismissed and looked around for a possible customer.

Mr. Hotchkiss, the minister, walked through the Sunday school room. Ellie liked Mr. Hotchkiss. He always treated her politely, as if she were grown up.

"Mr. Hotchkiss!" she called, running after him.

"Hello there." Mr. Hotchkiss put a hand on her shoulder.

"Mr. Hotchkiss," Ellie said breathlessly, "do you think a poor little mouse could have a comfortable home in the church?"

"Why," Mr. Hotchkiss said thoughtfully, "I've no doubt a mouse could have a most comfortable home here. In fact, the thought has occurred to more than one mouse, but I believe we've got rid of them all."

"B-b-but," Ellie stuttered in her eagerness, "I have a very nice mouse here—" she patted the box—"and I have to get rid of it on account of my sister Esther. And if it could live way, way down in the basement of the church, and the janitor would feed it—it wouldn't eat much, hardly anything—nobody would ever see it, and it would be such a good safe place for a mouse, Mr. Hotchkiss!"

"Well now, you see," Mr. Hotchkiss argued seriously, "the only trouble is that your mouse might not stay way, way down in the basement. And what do you think would happen if some nice old lady saw him scamper up the aisle and into her pew in the middle of service?"

"He wouldn't hurt her!" Ellie said disgustedly.

Mr. Hotchkiss shook his head and patted her shoulder again. "No, Ellie, it just wouldn't do. Now you keep right on liking mice and all things that creep upon the earth. But if I were you, I'd let that mouse out in a nice sunny field where he can enjoy life." Mr. Hotchkiss hurried off.

Esther and Andy had gone, but Janie was drawing pictures in the dirt with a stick when Ellie came out of Sunday school. She threw the stick away and trotted along. "Didn't anybody like Mouse, Ellie?"

"Oh yes, they liked him," Ellie said. "Only their mothers wouldn't let them, I guess. And," she shook her head seriously at Janie, "a church would not be a good home for a mouse, Janie. Mr. Hotchkiss said so."

"Oh," Janie said. They walked in silence.

"The best place is a nice sunny field where he can enjoy life," Ellie explained.

Janie asked, "Like the one we cross going to school?"

Ellie's face lighted up.

"Then maybe you'd see him sometimes," Janie suggested.

Ellie suddenly felt happier. The field was a whole block square, with a path cutting across it that all the children took, going to school. There were buttercups and daisies and black-eyed Susans and even a few wild raspberries growing in the field. It always smelled warm and sweet going through the high weeds in spring, and the sun poured down, hot and good. What a lovely place for a mouse to live, especially a mouse who had been shut up in a tin box.

Oh, how glad I am, Ellie thought, that Mr. Hotchkiss wouldn't let him go down in that dark, damp cellar!

"Come on, Janie, let's take him there right now!" she cried.

They pushed deep into the long green weeds at the side of the path. Ellie knelt down, pushed the cover from the tin box, and Mouse scrambled out. Instantly he was lost in the grass. Ellie and Janie looked, pulling the tangles aside. But Mouse had disappeared.

"Well," Ellie said finally, "I'll leave his box here." She arranged the long grass so it almost hid the box. No one would find it but Mouse. "He'll have something to come back to, and it'll seem like home to him. I don't think he'll be lonesome if he has his box, do you, Janie?"

Janie shook her curls. "And you can bring him some cheese every day on your way to school."

Ellie wasn't sure she could manage that every day. "But I will sometimes," she said, "and leave it in the box for a surprise."

They pushed back to the path through the weeds, stamping the dust from their black patent leather Sunday slippers.

"And I hope," Ellie said fiercely, casting one backward look in Mouse's direction, "that some day, when they're going to school, he'll jump right out and scare the wits out of those silly girls at the party!"

CHAPTER 6

MISS FRENCH TO THE RESCUE

In May the dogwood blossoms lay scattered like snowflakes over the front lawns, while plumes of purple lilac, snuggling against the houses in long hedges, reached for the blue sky. Tulips, in a dozen gay colors, stood guard along garden walks.

This morning Ellie was a bit later than usual

in starting for school. She had taken Rocky for his stroll, and spring had gone to Rocky's head. He had burrowed into the lilies of the valley and Ellie had quite a time finding him.

Esther and Andy and Janie had gone. Not a school child was anywhere in sight as Ellie headed up the street carrying her brief case. When she reached the vacant lot, however, she could see a group a long way ahead of her, almost at the other side of the field.

Just as she spied them, three figures broke out of the group and began to run. Shrill shrieks drifted back to Ellie from the fleeing figures. From the high sound of the yells she could tell they were girls, but she couldn't see who. Ellie began to run to catch up with them, whoever they were, and see what was going on.

Now she could make out Janie's bright blue jacket. Janie wasn't running. She seemed to be arguing with someone. Ellie was coming closer. She could see a cluster of boys around Janie.

What in the world was Janie doing? She seemed to be pulling on something. She was try-

ing to get something away from a boy. Suddenly
the boys began to run, Janie after them, waving
one arm wildly.

"Janie!" Ellie shouted. "Wait up!"

Janie stopped and looked back. She cast one
glance at the boys, who slowed down, laughing,
and then went along. Janie waited for Ellie.
Her cheeks were bright pink and her eyes sky-
blue as Ellie came up.

"What're you doing?" Ellie called.

"I've got something for you, Ellie!" Janie, in
her eagerness, ran to meet her friend.

"What?"

"Look!"

From Janie's hand dangled a small, limp snake.

"Where did you get it?" Ellie accepted the
snake with interest. Why, she thought with surprise, it feels warm! She had always supposed a
snake would be cold and clammy.

"Those boys," Janie explained, "found it in
the field and they were going to chase some dopey
girls with it—Lilac and some others—and the girls
ran away. And I wanted the boys to give it to

me so I could keep it for you. But they wouldn't.
So I just pulled and pulled and I got it! I didn't
hurt the snake," she told Ellie, her eyes round
and serious. "I pulled very carefully. And those
boys kept laughing, so I chased them and then
they ran, too."

Ellie was examining the light stripes on the
snake's brown back. It wriggled slightly in her
hand, and she turned it over and studied the
yellowish belly.

"Thank you, Janie, for getting it," Ellie said
thoughtfully. "I never had a snake before. It's
very interesting." She frowned. "What shall we
do with it?"

"Take it home and keep it?" Janie suggested.

Ellie considered, still admiring the snake. She
put her lips together firmly before she spoke.
"What I'd really like to do is take it home and
put it in my sister's drawer or something, like
Andy did with Rocky. She deserves to be scared
good and proper, making me get rid of Mouse!"

"Yes!" Janie agreed. "Why don't you do it,
Ellie?"

Ellie sighed. "No, my mother would take Esther's side." She shook her head sadly. "My mother always takes her side! And I don't think your mother would let you keep it either, Janie. Anyhow, we haven't got time to go home now. I'll just have to take it to school. Come on, Janie!"

They skipped and ran the rest of the way, the snake dangling from Ellie's hand. The bell hadn't rung yet. The school ground was filled with shouting, playing children. The girls in Ellie's class were clustered near the entrance around Lilac, Mary Anne, and Phyllis, who appeared to be the heroines of the moment.

"And we ran," Mary Anne gasped, rolling her eyes and clasping her hands, "until we nearly died!"

"My throat's sore, I screamed so much!" Phyllis declared.

"Look!" someone squealed as Ellie drew near. "Ellie's got the snake! Ellie's got the snake!"

The group broke up, some of the girls backing away from the snake with nervous squeals and giggles. As it happened, Lilac couldn't run. She was hemmed in on one side by the stone steps, on the other by a wall of the building. Her eyes fastened on the snake fearfully as Ellie approached, and she shrank back into the corner.

Ellie came closer to the group, eager to show the snake. She held it out.

"See him?" she cried proudly.

Lilac gave a screech and turned her face to the wall. "Take it away!" she gasped.

Ellie regarded Lilac. The snake writhed a little. Lilac pressed flatter against the wall, her face hidden in her hands. The sight of Lilac cowering before her only made Ellie disgusted and impatient. "Scaredy cat!" she said.

"Take it away!" Lilac begged desperately in a muffled voice. "Oh, please, Ellie, please!"

Ellie stood looking at her a moment longer. What could you do with a girl like that, anyhow? Ellie shrugged her shoulders and swung around. "Oh pooh!" she said, and flipped the snake carelessly forward over Lilac's shoulder as a parting gesture.

At the touch of the snake Lilac gave a loud shriek. Her arms flew up and beat the air wildly. She threw herself on the ground against the wall and screamed and screamed, kicking as if she still felt the snake and was trying to throw it off.

Children came running from all over the school ground. A teacher came hurrying up.

"Ellie scared her with the snake," Mary Anne explained.

"Go to your rooms—all of you," the teacher said, casting a hurried glance at Ellie and the snake. Slowly Ellie and the others climbed the steps, leaving the teacher to deal with Lilac.

When Ellie and her classmates got to their own room, everyone was eager to tell Miss French what had happened—all but Ellie, who still carried the snake and felt thoroughly disgusted with the rumpus Lilac had made. Lilac wasn't worth talking about, in Ellie's opinion.

"Oh dear!" Miss French said when she heard the story. She looked at Ellie reproachfully. "Ellie, it's a terrible thing to frighten anyone like that."

Ellie looked down, swinging the snake back and forth. "Lilac's a scaredy cat," she said stubbornly.

"But scaring her to death won't help," Miss French said.

"And anyway," Ellie added, "I didn't *mean* to scare her. I only wanted to show her the snake wouldn't hurt her!"

Miss French relented. "I'm sure you didn't really mean to," she said. "Well, what are you going to do with the snake now?"

Ellie looked up, feeling more cheerful. "Miss French, could I keep him here just for a little while?" she asked. "Because I'd like to watch him and see if he sheds his skin or anything like that."

"I think that would be interesting," Miss French agreed. "Let me see. What could we put him in?"

"A box?" Mary Anne suggested.

"Wouldn't a jar be better, so we could watch him?" Miss French asked. "Joey, run down and see if Mr. Dillon has a clean gallon jar he can lend us for a few days." Joey Curtis departed to find the janitor.

Lilac did not appear. A boy came and delivered a note to Miss French.

"Isn't Lilac coming?" Mary Anne asked curiously as the teacher folded the note.

Miss French shook her head. "Lilac has gone home. Now children, please, we'll just forget the whole thing."

Soon the snake was housed in a gallon jar, with a few rocks to crawl among. They set the jar on the broad window sill. All morning the children kept going over to take a look. By noon even the girls who had been most nervous were peering in at him with an easy curiosity. They had never seen a snake before so close up.

"Hey, maybe he's hungry," Joey suggested.

"What do snakes eat?" Ellie asked.

"Insects, I suppose," Miss French told them. "And I believe he'd eat chopped meat if you gave it to him. I'll tell you what, children. How would you like to learn all about garter snakes for your nature study?"

"Yes!" the class shouted.

Ellie could hardly believe her ears. Did Miss French mean she could leave the snake here? For keeps? It was too good to be true.

"We might even start a little zoo," Miss French went on. "Do any of you have anything else to contribute?"

"I have a red eft," Ellie said quickly. "He's home in a mayonnaise jar."

"All right, bring him in," Miss French said.

"I've got some goldfish."

"I know where there's a toad!"

Grade Three was chattering like a flock of excited birds, making suggestions for the zoo.

"Well, it looks as if we're well started," the teacher said, smiling at them.

Lilac did not appear for the afternoon session. "I called for her," Phyllis, who lived next door to Lilac, told the girls, "but her mother said when she had hys-hys-terics this morning on account of the snake it made her real sick. So her mother is going to keep her home from school for a few days."

That silly Lilac! Ellie thought. She acted crazier than Esther, even.

But Ellie had too many exciting things to think about to waste any more thought on Lilac. Skipping home from school across the field in the warm afternoon sunshine, she thought of Mouse. She always remembered Mouse when she passed the spot where his box lay hidden in the grass. Always until now the thought had made her sad. It reminded her of the dreadful fact that she could never, forever, have any little animals to watch and feed and play with and take care of.

But now when she thought of Mouse, instead of feeling bad Ellie's heart gave a thrilling little jump. Because maybe, now, she could really have some animals. A zoo in school! Oh boy, oh boy!

CHAPTER 7

THE ZOO

ELLIE carefully deposited the heavy paper-wrapped package on her desk. She put down her brief case and dropped the twig she was carrying.

"Oh boy!" she exclaimed, giving a sigh of relief. "My arms ache!" She stretched them out straight and wiggled her cramped fingers.

It was early—half an hour before time for school to start—but Ellie was not the first pupil to arrive. Mary Anne was there before her with two cigar boxes.

"What are they for?" Ellie asked, bending and stretching her tired arms.

"Insects. What've you got?"

"Some pieces of glass." Ellie began to undo the string around her package. "I asked the man at the camera store for them and he gave them to me. I'm going to make a house for Rocky."

Miss French had given them suggestions on how to make houses for the animals they hoped to have in their zoo. She was going to help them. She had told them they could work on the zoo during the last period of the day. They might also, if they wanted to, come to school early and stay late.

Ellie went over to the window to see the snake. "Good morning," she said to him, looking into the box. "You won't have to stay in there very long, because we're going to build you a nice house."

There was a scraping and bumping along the corridor as Joey Curtis came in, dragging an empty orange crate. Bob Epstein followed. Bob trailed a broomstick in one hand and in the other he clutched what looked to Ellie like an old curtain.

"What's that for?" she cried, pointing at the broomstick.

"Net," Bob said. "I'm going to make a net to catch insects."

"And I brought the cigar boxes to put the collection in, Bob," Mary Anne told him.

Ellie was still curious. "What're you going to do with the crate?" she asked Joe.

"Have it to put my sea shells in till we can build some better shelves or something."

Miss French came in. "Good morning," she said. "My goodness, what have we here?"

They clustered around her, all talking at once, and showed her what they had brought.

"That's just fine!" Miss French said. "Now, Mary Anne, you start cleaning the paper off your cigar boxes. Then you can sandpaper them and

stain them. Bob, did you get some holes bored in that broomstick?"

"Sure! Look. My father helped me."

"Good. Then make a loop of the wire you brought yesterday and we'll fasten the ends into the holes. When you get that fixed I'll show you how to sew the material to the wire to make a net."

"I brought a needle and thread," Bob said. "My mother threaded it." He felt in his pockets. "It's somewheres. Ouch!" he yelled. Hastily he pulled his hand from his pocket and shook it, inspecting the prick. Then he cautiously reached in the pocket again and extracted the needle and thread. "I found it," he said, grinning.

Miss French glanced at Ellie's glass plates. "You have quite a job ahead of you, Ellie," she said. "We'll have to tape those pieces together and use some aquarium cement on the inside.

"When you get all these houses made, you know," she told the children, "you'll have to furnish them."

"Animals don't need furniture!" Mary Anne

exclaimed, while Ellie watched Miss French's face doubtfully.

The teacher laughed. "Certainly they do! Some need water and some need dirt and moss and leaves, and some need sand or nice clean pebbles."

"Oh, that kind of furniture!" Ellie laughed.

"It will be a job to bring all those things in, just the same," Miss French told them.

"We don't mind," Ellie assured her.

"No! That's no work," Joey said.

Ellie had almost forgotten the twig on her desk. Now she remembered it and snatched it up. "Oh, Miss French," she said, handing it to her, "do you know what kind of insect nest that is, fastened to it?"

Miss French examined the strange little round ball firmly attached to the twig. "No, I don't recognize it." She held it up for the children to see. "Does anyone else know?" No one did.

"Let's keep it and see what happens," Miss French suggested.

"I know," Mary Anne said. "We ought to

have a special place to put things when we don't
know what they are."

"A what-is-it shelf?" Miss French asked.

"Yes! A what-is-it shelf!" they all cried.

When the bell rang and Miss French said, "All
right, children. At your desks now," a groan of
protest went up.

"Oh dear!" Ellie said. She was working at the
window sill, trying to fit pieces of glass together
and fasten them with tape, to make two sides of
Rocky's house. It was hard work. But she hated
to stop now. She sighed and laid the pieces
down.

"Hey, doesn't that look swell?" Joey stood
back and admired his own work. The orange
crate stood on end in a corner of the room, and
Joey's sea shells were laid out on the shelves in
neat array.

Usually Ellie went home for lunch, but today
she had brought sandwiches. There was a lunchroom in the school, but Ellie didn't want to waste
time going to it. Mary Anne and Phyllis had
brought their lunch, too.

"If we come early every morning and bring our lunch every noon and stay after school every day, it won't take hardly any time to get the zoo finished," Mary Anne said. She brushed away sandwich crumbs and began to peel her banana.

Ellie had just put some bits of roast beef from her sandwich in the snake's jar. She came back to her desk, took a cookie, and nibbled at it. "I can hardly wait!" she said. She put the whole cookie in her mouth and brushed the crumbs from her hands. "Come on, Phyllis. Let's work on Rocky's house now!"

Finally Miss French came back and shooed them out to get some fresh air.

Only a few children left when the closing bell rang that afternoon. "Aw heck!" Joey said, reluctantly picking up his books. "Who wants to take an old music lesson, anyhow!" He stamped off down the hall, thoroughly disgusted, then rushed back to stick his head in the door and yell, "Hey, maybe I'll come back afterward!" He dashed off, anxious to get the music lesson over as quickly as possible.

The others went on with what they were doing. Ellie was getting the pieces of glass together now, with Phyllis's help. Bob sat on the floor, scowling heavily and sewing the curtain material to the wire attached to the broomstick, the way Miss French had shown him.

"Oh boy," Phyllis said. "I'm tired! Let's rest a minute."

Ellie didn't want to rest. She didn't want to waste one second. But she couldn't go on alone, so she wandered around to see what progress the others were making.

Kenneth was punching holes with an ice pick in the tin top of a glass jar.

Ellie stooped to peer into the jar. "Is something in there?"

"Sure. Spider." He held up the jar so Ellie could see the spider spinning its thread from a twig. "When I get this done I'm gonna make a house for my caterpillar. And maybe a house for some ants, even!"

"Nuts!" Bob kicked his heels on the floor and shouted angrily. Ellie looked over at him.

"Thread broke!" Bob said crossly, holding it up and making a horrible face.

"You'll have to make a knot in it, Bob," Ellie told him. "Here, I'll show you." She went over and tried to roll the thread in her fingers to make a knot, as Mother had taught her, but Miss French finally had to come to the rescue.

"Children," Miss French said, straightening up when she had started Bob stitching again, "one thing we'll need is earthworms in a box of dirt, to feed some of these creatures you are planning to have. And we should have some meal worms and fish food, too."

"We've got lots of earthworms in our yard," Phyllis said. "I can dig some."

"So can I!" Bob shouted, without looking up from his sewing.

"All right. But meal worms and fish food have to be bought. And we'll need some money for other things too as we go along."

"I've got some money saved from my allowance," Ellie said quickly.

"No! I'll tell you," Mary Anne put in. "We

could each give some money from our allowance and put it all together to buy food and stuff for the animals."

"Yes, and we could put a box on your desk with a slot in the top, Miss French," Betty went on, "and put the money in the box."

"All right." Miss French smiled at their earnestness. "That would be just fine."

Ellie clapped her hands. "Goodie! We'll have lots of money to buy things for the zoo. Come on, Phyllis!" she called impatiently. "Let's work some more on Rocky's new house."

But Miss French glanced at her wrist watch. "My goodness," she exclaimed. "Do you know it's four-thirty? I'll have a lot of parents here looking for lost children if I don't send you all home this minute!"

CHAPTER 8

PICNIC AT FOREST FARM

THE third-grade girls were on their
way to a picnic. Phyllis Ainsworth had invited
everyone except Lilac, who was still away, to an
outdoor supper at Forest Farm this lovely Saturday in May. Forest Farm belonged to Phyllis's
mother.

Miss French and Miss Morgan, the principal of

the school, had been invited too. Mrs. Ainsworth was taking a load of children in her car and Miss Morgan was taking another in hers. They sat on top of one another but that was part of the fun. Ellie sat with Phyllis and her mother in the front seat as they rolled along a woodsy dirt road. In the back Miss French vainly urged four giggly third-graders to sit back quietly.

They had come a long distance on the highway first. In contrast with the broad, bare stretch of concrete this winding road was deep in cool shadows. Ellie sniffed the earthy smell.

"Oh!" she said, breathing a sigh of happiness, "it's nice here!"

"Wait till we get to the path through the woods!" Phyllis told her. "Mother, aren't we almost to the path?"

Mrs. Ainsworth nodded. "Yes. As a matter of fact," she said, peering ahead, "here we are right now!" She glanced in the mirror, put out her hand as a signal, and pulled the car off the road into a small clearing. Miss Morgan's car drew to a stop just behind.

"Let's get out and have a conference," Mrs. Ainsworth said. "It's a lovely walk to the house along this trail through the woods. By the road it's a couple of miles, but it's much shorter by the path. I thought some of you might like to walk."

"I'll go with them," Miss French said.

"And Mrs. Ainsworth and I will drive the cars around," added Miss Morgan, who had joined the group with the girls from the other car.

"Let's walk, let's walk!" Ellie cried, her eyes shining. Phyllis was already dancing ahead.

"Phyllis knows the way," Mrs. Ainsworth told them. "Just cross the bridge and keep going. The bridge is old but it's perfectly safe."

Ellie scampered after Phyllis. It felt wonderful to stretch her cramped legs here in the dim, cool woods.

"Stay together, girls," Miss French called after them.

But Phyllis was way ahead. "Here's the brook!" she shouted.

Now the brook gurgled gently beside them

between grassy banks. It was a friendly stream with big stones scattered through it. Phyllis was jumping from stone to stone. "Come on!" she called.

No third-grader could be expected to walk quietly along a path with those inviting stepping stones at hand. The girls hopped and jumped from one side of the brook to the other like grass-hoppers. They leaped along the middle of the stream from one boulder to the next. Squeals and laughter and shouts exploded like firecrack-ers in the quiet woods.

Ellie hopped and jumped madly, braids bob-bing. What fun this is, she thought, warm and breathless, balancing on one foot to measure the distance to the next rock.

"Girls," Miss French called from the path, "you'd better come back now. The brook is rougher down here."

Looking around from her rock in the middle of the water, Ellie saw that the stream was indeed wider and rockier and rushed along at a swifter pace. It was quite a bit below the level of the path now. Miss French stood looking down at them.

"O.K.," Ellie called, and made a flying leap for the bank. She landed on all fours, clutching the high grass. The others followed. They scrambled up the bank and gathered around Miss French.

"Any wet feet?" Miss French asked, looking down.

"No, Miss French!" they all assured her.

"Come along then. Let's see what else we can find."

The sun was low in the sky now. Here in the woods the early evening air felt cool and a strong smell of dampness rose from the rushing brook and the ferns and mosses. Ellie, walking with Mary Anne, suddenly stood still and listened.

"What's that?" she said.

"What?" Mary Anne asked, stopping too.

"That—that jingling."

"Oh, frogs, I guess," Mary Anne said. "Come on."

But Ellie stood still as the others went along.

Miss French caught up with her. "What is it, Ellie?"

"What makes that sound?" Ellie asked. "That —music, sort of?"

"Peepers," Miss French told her. "You find them in the spring wherever there's water. Isn't their song pretty?"

"Oh yes!" Ellie still stood there, entranced. "It sounds like—like—oh, just like lots of bells!"

As she spoke she imagined them. Tiny silver bells like the ones on a rocking horse that jingled as you rocked. Thousands of silver bells on the reins that someone was shaking, jingling the bells in that silvery little tune.

"Oh, Miss French," Ellie said breathlessly, "could we catch a peeper?"

"We might," Miss French said. "We can try after dark. You can usually find them with a flashlight. They keep right on singing when you turn the light on them. And you ought to see how the peeper's throat swells when he peeps!"

Ellie and Miss French were walking along slowly at the end of the straggling line. The group seemed to be slowing up. Miss French peered ahead.

"Here's the old bridge," she said.

The brook had widened and deepened now and rushed along below the path. Ahead of them a narrow wooden bridge crossed the stream. The girls were darting across the bridge with little squeals, then darting back again.

Miss French laughed. "There's not much left of the bridge, is there?" she said. It consisted of only a couple of wide planks with a gap between. There was no railing.

"Come on, Ellie!" Phyllis shouted. Phyllis was standing in the middle of the bridge and she was bobbing up and down to shake it. Every time she bobbed, the old planks heaved beneath her. Now Phyllis ran off the far side and left the bridge shaking. Everyone was across except Ellie and Miss French. The girls hopped and squealed with delight at Phyllis's daring.

"Hurry up across, Ellie!" Mary Anne yelled.

"O.K.," Ellie called back. "I'm coming." She ran ahead of Miss French.

But suddenly, at the edge of the bridge, a strange thing happened. Ellie stopped short. The planks seemed unexpectedly narrow to her. Looking at the unprotected sides made her stomach move with a sickening plunge. A wobbly feeling crept up Ellie's legs and set her knees shaking. It crept up and up. Her heart began to pound. Suddenly she gave a little gasp, turned, and dashed back to Miss French. She threw her arms around the teacher's waist and hid her face against her.

"Why, Ellie!" Miss French exclaimed. "What is it?"

"I don't want to cross the bridge!" Ellie's voice was muffled.

Across the bridge, sounding far away, Phyllis's voice called, "Come on, Ellie! Are you scared?"

Miss French spoke quietly after a moment. "It's all right, Ellie."

There was the patter of many feet as the girls raced back to surround Ellie and Miss French.

"What's the matter with Ellie?" Phyllis demanded.

"Nothing," Miss French said.

Ellie raised her face and sniffed back the tears.

"Then what are you crying for?" Mary Anne demanded, staring.

The tears came back and Ellie hid her face again.

"She just doesn't want to cross the bridge, that's all," Miss French said.

"Ellie's scared," one of the girls said with a giggle. Quickly the others took it up. "Ellie's scared, Ellie's scared!" they chanted.

"Stop it!" Miss French said sternly. "Stop it this minute!"

The chant died and after a minute Ellie cautiously raised her head again. She kept her eyes on the ground. In the group someone snickered.

"Phyllis, there's no other way of getting across, is there?" Miss French looked along the brook.

Phyllis shook her head. "No, you either have to cross the bridge or go back upstream and cross on the stones—only there isn't any path on the other side. Or else you have to go around by the road."

Miss French looked down. "We don't all want to go back, Ellie," she said. "I can't let you go back alone and jump the brook, and I hate to go with you and leave the others."

Ellie's heart, which had calmed down, began to flutter nervously again.

"Suppose I walk on one plank and you hold my hand and walk on the other," Miss French suggested.

Ellie hesitated a long moment. "All right," she said in a small voice. But she didn't look at the bridge.

"Go along, girls," Miss French said. "We'll follow you."

The girls scampered heedlessly across. "Now let's go," Miss French said. "We're all right, Ellie."

They started across. Below, miles below, it seemed to Ellie, rushed the dark stream capped with white foam. Suddenly Ellie's head was whirling. The whole woods, the whole world, was spinning crazily.

"I can't!" she gasped, terrified, standing still

and clutching Miss French's hand. "Come back, come back!"

They got back—how she didn't know. Far away, voices were taunting her again. "Ellie's afraid to cross the bridge! Ellie's afraid to cross the bridge!" Ellie didn't care. She felt only the exquisite relief of being on solid ground.

"Girls," Miss French called at last, "stay right where you are and wait for us."

She and Ellie went back up the path to the stepping stones, jumped across, and climbed up the farther bank. Ellie stumbled over roots and rocks after her teacher, arms outstretched for protection. Even so, the low branches pulled her hair and scratched her face. But at last they worked their way back to the clearing at the far side of the bridge, where the girls were waiting. Ellie pulled twigs from her disheveled hair and clothes and examined the scratches on her arms and legs.

"Well, here we all are," Miss French said cheerfully.

"My goodness, Ellie!" Mary Anne shook her

head. "I never thought you'd make such a fuss."

"Ellie's a scaredy cat!" someone said.

Ellie raised her chin and gazed off in the distance. "I don't care!" she said loftily, trying to sound as if she really didn't.

"We'll forget it now, girls," Miss French said.

But now that she was safely across, the girls' teasing suddenly seemed worse to Ellie than the bridge itself. The others all darted ahead. She walked quietly along with Miss French. The brook rippled innocently beside them once more. The awful feeling on the bridge seemed like an unreal dream. But the teasing stung and smarted inside her. "Ellie's scared, Ellie's scared!" The chorus of far-off taunting voices rang on and on in her ears.

But at last they came within sight of Forest Farm and Ellie forgot her troubles. Here was the silvery old house. Beyond the gentle slope of the lawn, blue hills rose across the valley.

"Look! Look!" Mary Anne was running down the yard. Ellie ran after her. Here was an apple tree, loaded with perfect blossoms. And beside it, holding its blooms high above their reach, grew the biggest lilac bush Ellie had ever seen.

The girls pulled down branches and stood on tiptoe to poke their noses into the fat, fragrant purple bunches. They sniffed and sniffed, never getting enough of the delicious perfume. They explored the grounds around the house, sampling the smells of all the lilac bushes like busy bees, calling one another to exclaim at each new blossoming tree or shrub.

The smell of wood smoke rose from the outdoor fireplace. It was time for supper. Miss French roasted hot dogs. Miss Morgan slit open the rolls. Mrs. Ainsworth dished out potato salad. They had pickles, too, and deviled eggs and cocoa, fruit and cookies.

The air felt cold now. The girls put on sweaters and coats. The orange coals glowed and blinked in the chilly dusk. White mist rose in the valley. The first star shone high in a clear sky. The loud whir of insects encircled them.

It was dark. The peeper song seemed more

insistent than ever. The girls moved closer to Mrs. Ainsworth and their teachers, closer to each other around the ruddy fire. Here and there a flashlight sent its beam through the night.

"Girls," Miss French said, "would you like to go down the path and see if we can find a peeper?"

"Yes!" Ellie cried, jumping up.

"Yes!" echoed a chorus. From still others came doubtful murmurs. The woods were dark and damp. They preferred to stay safe and cozy around the fire.

"Bring your flashlights," Miss French said, "and some paper cups. Just follow my light."

Ellie was right behind Miss French. As they entered the woods, the peeper chorus grew suddenly loud. It seemed just ahead. She flashed her light around on the ground, but she could see no singers and the chorus still beckoned her on like a will-o'-the-wisp. Now the brook joined them, unseen, and sang its song in the dark.

"Ooh, Ellie, I'm scared!" Mary Anne whispered, just behind her.

But Ellie felt excited and thrilled by the dark-
ness, so filled, she was sure, with tiny creatures.
She wished she could say to all the small things
hiding close to her, "Don't be afraid! I'll never,
never hurt you."

Suddenly a loud *peep* rose quite close to Ellie.
She stopped and flashed her light in the direction
of the sound. A second peep answered the first.
The girls scurried past, keeping as close to their
teacher as they could.

Ellie stood still and listened. *Peep*. Right
across the brook. She searched the ground with
her light. But in all those dry leaves how could
you ever see a little peeper?

Peep. At least the peeper wasn't running
away. It was across the brook, all right, and she
had to get over. Ellie located a stepping stone.
The edges of the stream were soft and muddy
and her foot slipped, but she got across and up
on the dry bank.

Peep. It was still across the brook, for at this
point the stream divided, one branch curving
sharply to the right. Ellie's flashlight covered

the opposite bank, inch by inch. *Peep, peep, peep.* She moved the light beam over the shallow water.

Peep, peep. The peeper seemed to be asking a question. "I won't hurt you," Ellie whispered, her light searching the ground. The beam moved up the bank again, into the leaves. Then sharply she turned it back to the edge of the water. Something had moved—something . . .

Ellie gave a little indrawn gasp of wonder. She saw it—under a rotten limb right at the edge. An unbelievably tiny frog with black, shiny eyes, pulsating with peeps that were bigger than he was, a huge rainbow bubble under his chin.

"Miss French, Miss French!" Ellie called as softly as she could, so excited, so fearful of losing him she did not know what to do first. "I've found one! Come quick!"

The flashlights down the stream turned in her direction. Miss French came back along the path, jumped the brook, and stood beside Ellie, pointing her light.

"There!" Ellie whispered.

"Yes. You'll have to get across to reach him. Put your light down. And wait till I get out the paper cups."

Ellie laid her flashlight in the grass and took a flying leap across the water. Miss French kept the peeper in the beam of her light. "Hurry now," she said, "before he jumps."

Ellie had to step down in the mud, one foot half in the brook, but she hardly noticed. Nothing mattered now but to encircle the peeper with her two hands before he took fright. He had stopped peeping. His bulgy little eyes stared straight ahead in the glare of the light.

"That's right," Ellie heard the teacher say. "One hand in back of him."

She had him! Inside her cupped hands she felt a flutter. She stood up. Miss French held out the cup. Ellie dropped the peeper inside.

"Have you got him? Is he in there?" The girls clustered around, clamoring. Ellie jumped back over the brook in a seventh heaven of joy. She had caught a peeper! She had seen him peep! She still couldn't believe it.

"Good work, Ellie!" Miss French said. "I'll put this other cup over him. Take a few wet leaves along."

Ellie took the two paper cups from the teacher to carry back. They seemed so light she felt a twinge of doubt. "Are you sure he's there?" she asked anxiously.

"He's there, and don't look now or he'll jump out."

The procession of flashlights moved back along the path, back into the firelight. The girls were all eager to see the peeper. Mrs. Ainsworth found a glass jar in the house and punched holes in the tin top with a can opener. With the girls pressing close around her, Ellie transferred the peeper to the jar.

"Oh, isn't he darling!" Mary Anne gasped.

Even Ellie was not prepared for anything so tiny. Why, the little brown thing wasn't an inch long! There he sat on his haunches, eyes staring, heart beating in his throat.

"Oh, give him to the zoo, Ellie!" Phyllis begged.

"What's his name going to be?" someone asked.

Ellie's head was bent over the jar. Suddenly the peeper's throat swelled. *Peep,* he sang bravely, but with that question in his song.

How could that big, strong, sturdy peep come from that tiny peeper? Ellie's heart went out to the small captive, singing with such courage in a strange new world. What was he trying to ask her? Oh, you know I'm your friend, don't you, Ellie told him with her thoughts.

"Yes, I am going to give him to the zoo," she said. "I'm going to fix a nice house for him, where he'll be happy."

His name? There's only one name for him, Ellie thought, only one.

"His name is Silver Bell!" she said.

CHAPTER 9

LILAC IS BACK

BY late May the little zoo in Grade
Three was a flourishing institution. Cages and
glass houses crowded the window sill. The snake
was there and seemed happy in an apple crate
with a hinged screen on one side. The crate was
furnished with rocks and the snake had his shallow dish of water.

The red eft had moved from Ellie's bedroom to the new, roomy house she had made. Silver Bell had a glass house too, with water in the bottom, leaves and rocks to sit on, and a small branch for climbing. He stayed hidden all day between two brown leaves, but now and then his clear, high peep rang out. The children never could catch Silver Bell in a peep. Ellie was glad she had seen his silvery bubble that night in the woods.

There was an aquarium where bright-hued tropical fish flashed through the water and snails drifted at snail's pace. A frog and a toad shared a glass house filled halfway up with black dirt and moss, and small turtles had a tank of their own with water for swimming and rocks for sitting.

But the prize possession of Grade Three was a pair of hooded rats, given by the pet shop where they bought their meal worms and equipment they could not make. White and soft-furred, with pink eyes and ears, a wide collar and back stripe of palest beige, and tails longer than their bodies, Jack and Jill were gentle and lovable. They quivered with eagerness to be lifted from their cage, cuddled and stroked by kind hands.

Ellie adored them. They were like the white bunny rabbits she had always yearned for. Nestling Jill in the curve of her arm, Ellie understood the difference between these pets and Mouse. Jack and Jill trusted people. They would be helpless turned out into a field. But Mouse belonged outdoors. Mouse was a wild thing who believed human beings were his enemies.

Ellie loved to pour milk for Jack and Jill. She hung over them to see the little creatures lap the milk with small tongues, just like pussy cats.

Joey's shells were housed now, along with a butterfly collection, in an old bookcase that someone's mother had found in the attic. Ellie didn't like dead butterflies, however pretty their bright colors and patterns. She loved butterflies alive, even the plain yellow ones fluttering over flowers.

Some of the children, who did not care for animals or collections, were raising plants. A

carrot was putting forth feathery leaves in the
sunny window. A sweet potato in a tall vase was
growing both ways—roots down into water, vine
up in the air. A small white turnip pushed up
yellow-green, bushy leaves that looked good
enough to eat.

Outdoors the world was at its loveliest, with
roses and iris in fragrant blossom. Bees buzzed
in the heavy sweetness of syringa. Overnight, it
seemed, the great maples along the street, so slow
in unfolding their red buds, had grown leaves
that met and formed a green tunnel blocks long.

One Monday morning Ellie got to school early.
Mary Anne was there before her. As monitors
of the zoo, they had a great deal of work. The
janitor fed the animals over the week end. But
fresh paper had to be cut in strips for Jack and
Jill to sleep in. Dishes must be washed and filled
with water, fresh water added to the aquariums,
meal worms scooped out of their jar, earthworms
dug up. The snake needed chopped meat. A
fly, caught in cupped hands, went to the red eft.

Ellie flew busily around, carrying dishes to be

rinsed, bringing water from the cooler, opening the container of milk.

"I believe Jill's been lonesome!" she exclaimed, lifting the little thing out and cuddling her.

Mary Anne was holding the snake in one hand. "Hey," she exclaimed, surveying his length, "I think he's bigger!"

The bell rang and Ellie put Jill back and hurried to feed the frog and the toad. She felt bubbly with happiness this morning. It was wonderful to get back to the animals! Ellie hadn't known what to do with herself those two long days away from school.

The pupils began to come in. Miss French was at her desk now. Boys and girls clustered around the animals, taking them out of their houses, talking to them.

Ellie, putting the top on the terrarium where the frog and toad lived, heard Miss French say, "Why, Lilac dear, I'm so glad to see you!"

Lilac had been out ever since the day when Ellie had brought the snake to school. Her mother had told Miss French the fright had so upset her that it seemed best to take her away for a while.

Ellie spun around as Miss French spoke. Oh good, she thought, Lilac hasn't seen the zoo! More than anything, Ellie and the others loved to show off their zoo.

"Hello, Lilac!" Ellie cried, running toward her. She forgot Lilac's fear of snakes and her own impatience. So much had happened since then. There was so much to show and to tell.

"Do you feel all right now?" Phyllis inquired.

The children clustered around Lilac.

"Your face is all tan!" Mary Anne said admiringly.

"I've been to the seashore," Lilac explained, "and we sat on the beach every day."

"Lilac"—Ellie couldn't wait—"we've got a surprise for you!"

"A zoo!" Joey said promptly.

"With real animals!" one of the other boys assured her.

A strange expression crept over Lilac's face.

"Only they can't get out," Ellie added quickly. She had suddenly remembered about the snake. But surely, she thought, Lilac isn't afraid of animals in cages.

"Come on, Lilac, come see them!" Mary Anne seized Lilac's hand.

"What—what kind of animals?" Lilac pulled her hand from Mary Anne's. Her eyes traveled fearfully toward the zoo collection in the window. She clutched Miss French's desk.

"Oh, darling hooded rats!" Ellie cried joyfully.

The children all talked at once.

"And turtles."

"Come on, Lilac, come on!"

"And a frog and a toad!"

"And a snake!" Whoever said that, like Ellie, had completely forgotten Lilac's sad adventure with that very same snake.

The nice color suddenly drained from Lilac's face, leaving it deathly white. She clapped one hand over her mouth. Above the hand her eyes were wide with horror. With a small gasp Lilac turned and ran from the room.

"Lilac!" Miss French got up from her desk. The children crowded after her into the hall.

Lilac was sobbing, with Miss French's arms around her.

"I—can't—help—it!" Lilac gasped between sobs.

"But Lilac," Miss French protested, "the snake is harmless. He can't get out anyway, and you needn't go near him."

"Ugh!" Lilac's face was hidden. A shudder went over her.

Miss French stood patting her back. Lilac grew quieter. "There now," Miss French said, "you come back."

Lilac pulled away. "But I hate toads—and frogs—and rats!" Her voice rose in a wail. "I'm not going to stay in the same room with all those —nas-ty—things!" Lilac began to cry wildly again.

After a minute Miss French spoke to the children over Lilac's head. "All right, children," she said. "You may take the zoo into Miss Morgan's office. Put the animals on the big table. Lilac, come into the teachers' room."

Ellie watched Miss French lead Lilac, her shoulders still jerking with sobs, down the hall. Then she turned slowly to Mary Anne. The pupils of Grade Three looked at one another. There were no smiles or giggles. Only grim silence.

Ellie turned without a word and went back into the room. The others followed.

Phyllis whispered, "She's really scared!"

"She didn't even look at them," Joey said.

"Why is she afraid when they can't get out?" Mary Anne asked, puzzled.

But Ellie was already picking up the smaller aquarium.

"Hey, do you think we really have to take them?" Joe said doubtfully. "Maybe Miss French will get her calmed down."

"If she'd only *look* at Jack and Jill and see how sweet they are!" Mary Anne began.

Ellie, carrying the aquarium, shook her head. "No, it's no use, Mary Anne. I know on account of my sister. We'll just have to take them to Miss Morgan's office."

"Even the fish?" Phyllis asked.

"Yes," Ellie told her grimly, "you'd better take everything that's alive."

The boys carried the terrariums and the other aquarium. The girls transferred the snake and the worms.

Now only the rats were left. Ellie took out first Jill and then Jack, to hold each one gently. "Never mind," she murmured into the pink ears, "I'll take care of you and visit you just the same!"

But it wouldn't be the same. Ellie knew that the principal couldn't have thirty boys and girls —no, twenty-nine—running in and out of her office all day to visit their pets.

She put Jack and Jill back and fastened the cage. Then she glanced around, determined to be thorough. Was there anything else? Shells and birds' nests and butterflies. Would Lilac be scared of dead butterflies, she wondered in disgust. The insect nest Ellie had found sat on the what-is-it shelf. Ellie's eyes rested on it for a moment but she decided it was harmless.

She picked up the rats' cage. Her lips tightly

set, Ellie carried the light burden down the hall.

Was the same thing going to happen at school that happened at home? Couldn't they have the zoo, just because one girl was scared of it? Couldn't she *ever* have any animals?

It isn't fair! It just isn't *fair,* Ellie stormed to herself.

Lilac and Miss French came back and the class settled down. Lilac's eyes were red. She didn't look at any of the children and they stared at her curiously.

Miss French did not mention the zoo again, except to ask Ellie and Joey and Mary Anne to look in at the animals at noon and after school. But Ellie, thinking of little else all day, made up her mind to speak to Miss French. She lingered after school.

"Yes, Ellie?" the teacher said, turning to her.

"Miss French," Ellie began, "do we have to keep the zoo in Miss Morgan's office all the time?"

Miss French hesitated. "I don't know yet, Ellie."

"But Lilac's going to spoil everything!" Ellie burst out fiercely.

The teacher didn't answer. She picked up a pencil and made some marks on her pad.

"And I think it's mean of her!" Ellie stormed.

"You're the one who's mean, I'm afraid," Miss French said quietly, not looking up.

Ellie stared. *"I'm* not mean," she said.

"Yes, Ellie, you are, even though you don't intend to be."

"But I didn't do anything." Ellie was astonished at Miss French. "I . . ."

"Ellie," the teacher said, "were you being mean when you wouldn't cross the bridge?"

"No! They were mean to me!"

"You were terribly frightened, weren't you?" Miss French asked.

Ellie nodded.

"Well, that's how Lilac feels about snakes. And when you tell her she's a scaredy cat, and when you fling a snake at her, you're just as mean as the girls at the bridge when they made fun of you."

"B-but," Ellie stammered, "I thought—I didn't mean—I d-didn't know she felt—like *that!*"

"Some people are afraid of shaky bridges, Ellie, and some are afraid of snakes. Some people are afraid of other things. But now that you know how it feels, I hope you'll never be unkind to Lilac again or anyone else who is frightened." Miss French stood up. "Now run along." She patted Ellie's shoulder. "We'll have to see what we can do about the zoo."

Ellie walked home by herself, stunned and quiet. She felt quite shaken by what Miss French had said. Did Lilac really feel like that when she just saw a little snake? All shaky, with her head whirling and her heart thumping and everything spinning around inside of her and out?

As she thought about it the feeling came back —that dreadful feeling on the bridge. Well, Ellie thought, I guess we can't have the zoo. I guess we just can't have it if it makes Lilac feel so awful. I never knew that was how the snake made her feel.

And with the bridge feeling another memory

returned—the sound of those far-off taunts.
"Ellie's scared, Ellie's scared!" Even now the
memory made Ellie feel sick inside.

Suddenly a feeling of shame crept over her. I
was just as mean as those girls, she thought.
Lilac can't help being scared.

Ellie's last thought before going to sleep that
night was of Lilac and the zoo. In her dreams all
the children were chasing one another with the
animals. Once she cried in her sleep and woke
up. She sat up, missing Pete's weight at her feet.

But Pete was standing beside the narrow bed,
just standing quietly, close to her in the dark as if
to say, "I'm here." His breath was warm and
doggy. Ellie put her arms around his shaggy
neck and laid her cheek against his muzzle. Pete
kissed her.

At least I've got Pete, Ellie thought with a
comforted sigh as she snuggled back into the
pillow.

CHAPTER 10

DRAGONS WITH DARK EYES

IT was raining when Ellie awoke next morning. She lay watching the downpour outside her window and listening to the mutter of thunder. Ellie shut her eyes as lightning made the gloomy morning bright and turned slanting sheets of rain to yellow.

Gradually the events of the day before returned. Lilac. The zoo. Oh dear, Ellie thought dismally, staring at the rain. What fun is school anyhow, with the zoo way down in Miss Morgan's office!

Everything went wrong this morning. Her shoelace broke. She wasted five minutes trying to tie the pieces together and finally clumped down to Mother, extremely cross, carrying the shoe.

At breakfast she spilled egg on her clean dress. Scooping it up only made the spot worse.

"You'd better change your dress, Ellie," Mother said.

"No!" Ellie jerked away.

"Why, Ellie!" Mother said, looking at her. "You're not usually a cross little girl."

Then Ellie couldn't find her reading book. By the time Mother located it behind a cushion on the davenport, Esther was calling, "Ellie! If you want to ride, hurry up. Daddy can't wait all day."

"I don't care whether I go or not!" Ellie muttered, pulling on her rubber boots. When

Mother thrust her raincoat around her and put her bag in her hand, Ellie walked deliberately, instead of running out to the car.

"Don't hurry, your Majesty," Andy remarked. Ellie climbed in beside him without speaking and let him pull the door shut.

"What's the matter? Get out the wrong side of bed?" Andy inquired.

Ellie stared out of the window without replying.

Daddy dropped Andy and Esther at their entrance to the school and drove Ellie around to hers. She took her time going up the walk. She didn't care if she *was* late. She didn't care about anything. Glumly she climbed the stairs.

But as she reached the second floor and pulled open the door into the corridor, Ellie stopped in surprise.

The door of Grade Three classroom, halfway down the hall, was swarming with children. They were trying to see into the room, squealing, pushing. All the second floor seemed to be there. From inside came surging an uproar such as Ellie had never before heard in the school corridors.

What had happened? Ellie began to run. One of the girls in the door, a fourth-grader, recognized her and began to yell, "Hurry up, hurry up!"

"What is it?" Ellie shoved through the crowd of children.

"It's a cocoon!"

"It's worms!"

"It's butterflies!"

Apparently Grade Three had completely lost its mind. Children were standing on chairs and reaching up on the wall. They stood on desks pushed over to the wall. They stood on tiptoe. Children were darting to Miss French's desk, putting something in a box, and darting away again. Every single child, Ellie saw, was carrying a soupspoon!

"What is it?" she gasped again.

"Oh, Ellie!" Mary Anne paused, spoon in hand, long enough to explain breathlessly. "It's praying mantises! They hatched out. Look, they're all over everywhere!"

Ellie turned in bewilderment to Miss French. As she did so, Lilac came in, gave a sudden gasp at the sight, and stopped short at the door.

"The nest you brought in, Ellie," Miss French said, accepting another donation to her box. "It hatched out. They're praying mantises—hundreds of them. We're getting all we can and putting them in this box. Hurry and help, Ellie. Take a spoon and scoop them off the wall."

At last Ellie took it in. Her eyes roved over the walls. Sure enough, they were covered with the tiniest clinging, crawling things—swarms and swarms of them on the walls, the desks, the ceiling, the window shades. Ellie gasped.

Behind her, Lilac saw the praying mantises too. Ellie heard a stifled cry and turned to see Lilac scurry into the hall for safety. But this time neither the children nor Miss French paid any attention.

Ellie dumped her raincoat and brief case on the nearest desk and hastily yanked off her boots. "Where's a spoon?" she cried.

Someone thrust one into her hand. They were

lunchroom spoons, Ellie noticed. Then, standing on tiptoe, she carefully scooped a baby praying mantis into her hand.

Beside her, Joey said, "Don't hurt them."

As if she would! Ellie gave him a withering
sidelong look. She held the baby in her hand
and studied the tiny body, not much larger than
a fly, and the great dark staring eyes. It looked
exactly like a big praying mantis only it had no
wings and was honey-colored instead of green.
It's a dragon, Ellie thought wonderingly, a tiny,
tiny dragon.

Ellie worked feverishly, carrying baby after
baby to the box. And still they were everywhere.
The bell rang and children from other classes
were herded away into their rooms by the teachers. Grade Three was left alone with its baby
praying mantises and its busy spoons.

Ellie paused, spoon in hand, to catch her
breath. Mr. Dillon, the janitor, had brought a
stepladder and the boys were taking turns climbing it to reach the babies on the upper walls and
ceiling. Ellie watched them. Miss Morgan had

come in and was talking to Miss French as she stood looking around.

Suddenly Ellie noticed Lilac hovering just outside the door. Ellie thought, She wants to come in but she doesn't dare. Like I didn't dare cross the bridge.

Joey Curtis, descending the ladder with a box top full of praying mantises, saw Lilac too. He held out the box with an impish grin. "Here's something for you, Lilac," he said. Lilac jerked back quickly.

Ellie jumped suddenly to her feet and ran over to Joey. "Joey," she whispered so Lilac couldn't hear, "don't tease her! She can't help it if she's afraid of bugs and snakes."

Joey glanced at her in surprise. "O.K.," he said good-naturedly and climbed back up the ladder.

"Come on, Ellie! Help!" Mary Anne cried, and Ellie went back to work.

Miss Morgan came back after a while. There were two men with her. One carried a camera.

"Children," Miss Morgan said, "this is **Mr.**

Johnson, a reporter from the *Daily Star*. And
this is Mr. Smith, the photographer. He wants
to take some pictures and Mr. Johnson wants to
find out all about the praying mantis nest so he
can put it in the paper."

Mr. Smith took some pictures of the baby
praying mantises and of the nest, now looking
like a deserted honeycomb with a little tassel of
white silk dangling from it. He took a picture
of the children scooping the babies off the wall.

Ellie was in that picture. As she stood with
the others, facing the camera, her eyes roved to
Lilac, watching them from the other side of the
room. Lilac looked lonesome. As if she wished
she could be in the picture with them, Ellie
thought.

Mr. Johnson asked who had brought the nest
to school. Ellie raised her hand and Mr. Smith
took a picture of her all alone. He asked her
where she found it and whether she liked animals. That started the children talking about
the zoo. Mr. Johnson wrote down everything
they said.

Then the two men asked Ellie and Mary Anne and Joe to come with them to Miss Morgan's office. They took pictures of the children holding the various animals.

By the time the men left, the rain had stopped. The sun, hot now in a sapphire sky, was rapidly drying the pavements and turning a million flashing drops in the grass to rainbows.

"Children," Miss French said, "have we got them all?"

They peered around the room. Every praying mantis baby appeared to be in captivity.

"Then," Miss French said, "suppose we keep one to watch for a while and let the others go."

"But they can't fly," Ellie protested.

"They'll crawl away and their wings will grow," Miss French assured her. Carefully she scooped up a spoonful of babies and carried them to an open window, the children crowding around. A vine spread up from the ground and over the sill. Miss French blew gently on the baby mantises and they drifted down into the vine and disappeared from sight.

The children turned most of the babies loose
in the vine. They took the rest down at noon
and shook them out on the hedge that sur-
rounded the school grounds.

By afternoon they all felt well acquainted with
the one remaining mantis infant—all but Lilac,
who kept far away. The young mantis appeared
perfectly at home. Ellie set him on a pencil as
the children clustered around, and the tiny thing
reared up as if saying its prayers and watched
Ellie with big black eyes in a pointed face.

"Hey, it can turn its head around!" Joey cried.

"Oh, it's cute!" Ellie exclaimed. She forgot
Lilac. "Can't we keep him for a pet, please, Miss
French?"

But Miss French read to them from a book
how a young praying mantis disappears to hide
until its body is green to match the leaves and its
wings have grown.

"It would be kinder to let it go," Miss French
told them. "Besides, it's against the law to keep
a praying mantis. They destroy many harmful
insects."

So Ellie carried out the last praying mantis when she left school and placed it carefully in the hedge. None of its brothers and sisters was in sight. She hoped it would find some of them.

The pictures and story were in the paper the next night, right on the front page. Ellie had told the family about it, and Esther was there to pounce on the paper the minute it thudded on the porch from the paper boy's bicycle. She read the story standing. Andy read it over her shoulder. Then Mother sat down to read it and Ellie read it over her shoulder.

"Well!" Mother said. "My little girl is famous!" She put her arm around Ellie.

Ellie finally got the paper to herself and sat on the front steps to study the pictures. She read the account slowly and carefully.

Mr. Johnson had got it all right. The story told how Ellie had found the nest in the field. It told how the zoo had started with the snake Ellie had taken to school, and about Jack and Jill and Rocky and how Ellie had found Silver Bell with her flashlight.

The story told where Ellie lived and mentioned Mother and Daddy and Esther and Andy, and even Pete and Mister.

It gave the names of several children in the class, but not Lilac. Miss French was quoted as saying the zoo had temporarily been moved to the principal's office "for various reasons."

Ellie heard Mother phone Daddy and ask him to pick up some extra copies of the paper on his way home. She wanted to send them to the uncles and aunts.

Then the phone rang and it was a friend of Andy's. Ellie, on the front steps with the paper, raised her head as she heard Andy say, "Hey, did you see the paper? That's my sister, you know."

Why, Ellie thought, she'd never heard Andy call her "my sister" in that proud way before. Usually he said "my kid sister," or "It's only El."

Esther came out on the porch. "Want to come with me for a soda, Ellie?" she asked.

Ellie scrambled up. "O.K. I'll get my money."

"Don't bother," Esther said. "I'll treat you."

Ellie looked at her in astonishment. Esther hardly ever asked her to go anywhere, to say nothing of treating. Well . . . Ellie beamed as she skipped beside her sister.

It certainly was nice to be treated so politely by her family and to be sitting on a stool in the drugstore eating a fudge sundae with nuts and whipped cream and a cherry. Ellie almost lost the anxious feeling that lay within her like a heavy weight. Almost. She could not quite get rid of the unhappy thought that, because Lilac was afraid of animals, they would probably have to give up the zoo.

CHAPTER 11

THE LAST DAY

FOR the next few days people kept stopping Ellie on the street and saying, "Aren't you the little girl who found the praying mantis nest?"

Ellie was always pleased that folks were interested in the baby praying mantises and the zoo. She got to school early every morning to look after the animals. She and some of the others went to the principal's office again at noon and after school. Sometimes Miss Morgan was having a meeting and looked up with a frown when they came in. They tiptoed and whispered and kept as quiet as third-graders could. Still, Ellie felt uncomfortable about bothering Miss Morgan all the time. She was sure this arrangement couldn't go on forever.

She and Mary Anne discussed it one day, loitering home in the afternoon sunshine.

"Prob'ly Miss Morgan'll let the zoo stay there till vacation," Mary Anne said. There was only a week of school left. "Then prob'ly we won't have it next year."

"I guess not," Ellie said unhappily, her eyes on the ground.

"The heck with Lilac, anyhow!" Mary Anne exploded.

Ellie looked up. "But I know how she feels," she said. "She can't help it, Mary Anne. When you're very scared of something you just can't help it."

"Well, I think it's a shame!" Mary Anne muttered.

It was a day or so later when Miss Morgan came in. "May I speak to the class, Miss French?" she asked.

Ellie suddenly felt a little sick. This is it, she thought. Miss Morgan's going to tell us. She's going to say we can't have the zoo next term.

Thirty pairs of eyes were fixed on the principal. "Children"—Miss Morgan looked around, smiling—"do you know you're quite famous?"

The boys shuffled their feet in pleased embarrassment. The girls exchanged looks and giggled silently behind their hands.

"I've had letters," Miss Morgan said, "from all sorts of people who would like to contribute something to your collection. Other principals have called to ask if their children may come and see the zoo."

The class was quiet now, listening. "So," Miss Morgan went on, "Miss French and I have been talking. We're wondering if next year you would like to expand your collection and make it a sort of nature center where children from other schools can come and see the animals."

Ellie's heart leaped and began a loud thump-thumping in her ears. Miss Morgan's voice sounded far away. Am I dreaming she's saying this, Ellie wondered.

"How many of you would like that?" Miss Morgan said.

Twenty-nine hands shot upward. No, thirty. Ellie saw Lilac hesitate. Then her hand crept up timidly. Lilac wasn't going to be left out.

"All right," Miss Morgan said, "here's what we have in mind. Across the hall there's a room that's being used as a storeroom. It joins the classroom next to it. We'll move you into that classroom in September, and clean out the storeroom to use for the nature room."

Grade Three clapped and shouted until Miss Morgan motioned for silence. "You see," she said over the uproar, "if a pupil isn't interested, he needn't have anything to do with the nature room. And when visitors come they won't disturb the whole class.

"Best of all"—Miss Morgan smiled at the children, then at Miss French—"Miss French is going to stay with this class next year."

There was such a tumult this time that Miss Morgan put her hands over her ears, shook her head, laughing, and slipped out of the door. Miss French tried to calm the class. But she was just as excited as they were; anyone could see that.

"It's a good thing," Miss French said when she could make herself heard, "that this is the last week of school! I can see I won't get any work out of you. But next year," she went on, becoming serious, "I'll expect extra good work of my boys and girls. Will you promise me the nature room will improve your work—not hurt it?"

"Yes, Miss French!" they roared at her.

"Good. Now," Miss French said, "about vacation. We've got to arrange for the animals to be taken care of. Who would like to look after a pet at home this summer?"

Hands waved wildly again. Ellie's hand went up with the others, flapped, then slowly came down as she remembered. She couldn't take a pet home because of Esther.

One by one the children chose the animals they wanted for the summer. Jack and Jill first. If I could just have Jill, Ellie thought. But Esther . . . No, it would never do. Then the turtles, the toad, the fish were chosen.

"Miss French, may I have Rocky?" Bob asked.

"Rocky is Ellie's pet," the teacher reminded him.

Ellie spoke slowly. "I don't mind," she said. "You can have Rocky, Bob." She was remembering Esther's scream that time Rocky got in the silver drawer. And she knew now how Esther felt.

"How about the snake, Ellie?" Miss French was asking. "He was your find."

"Oh, no!" Ellie shook her head quickly. "I couldn't take him home."

Finally they decided to return the snake and Silver Bell to their homes out of doors.

The last week of school slipped along. This was summer at its loveliest. Ellie stared dreamily from the window at the full green trees swaying tirelessly against a radiant sky, at shadows dancing on green lawns. Such a drowsy vacation feeling drifted in the open windows on the warm breeze that Ellie would gladly have prolonged these last few days. She dreaded the long summer.

The last morning of school the children begged to have the zoo brought back. "Please, Miss French, can't we play with them just a little while?"

Ellie noticed that Miss French did not look in Lilac's direction as she said, "Very well. We'll have a farewell party."

Joyfully they rushed to lug back the cages and glass houses. Lilac did not offer to help. But neither, this time, did she run from the room. She sat, rather pale, her hands tightly clenched, and watched as the zoo houses crowded the window sill.

"Aw, Jill!" They crowded around as Ellie opened the screen and lifted out the snowy little creature. Eager hands reached to stroke Jill. Ellie's head bent over her as Jill snuggled her nose contentedly into the crook of Ellie's arm.

Phyllis was holding Jack now. The children transferred their attention to him. Joey had Rocky out. Mary Anne was looking for Silver Bell among the leaves. Grade Three, in half a dozen admiring circles, buzzed and chattered with affectionate enthusiasm. These were their friends, now to be parted from the class for three long months.

Ellie stood holding Jill, gently running her finger down the velvety back. Then, as she felt someone at her elbow, she glanced up. It was Lilac. Lilac's eyes were big as she gazed down at Jill. "I didn't know," Lilac said rather breathlessly, "they were white!"

"They're hooded white rats. See?" Ellie pointed out the faint beige hood. "Here," she said impulsively, "hold her!"

Lilac started back in alarm as Jill's long tail came into view. Ellie protested. "Lilac, she's so kind! Look!" She held her finger up to Jill's mouth. Jill sniffed delicately. "Please, Lilac, just hold her!"

At first when Lilac's hand closed cautiously around Jill and the white rat crept up her arm, Ellie thought Lilac was going to drop her, to say, "Ugh!" Ellie put out her hand quickly.

"Here, hold her like this." She showed Lilac how. Lilac still held Jill awkwardly. Then as she seemed to sense the helplessness of the small creature, Lilac began to relax. Her other hand stole up and smoothed Jill's coat.

"Oh," Lilac whispered, looking down at Jill, "she's nice, isn't she!"

Ellie hesitated a moment, then flew across the room. "Miss French, Miss French!" she cried softly. "Come look! Lilac's holding Jill!"

The children crowded around Lilac and Jill, proud and excited.

"Now you won't be afraid of the animals any more, will you?" Mary Anne said.

Miss French said hastily, "Now, now. Lilac's made a fine start. Don't rush her. Lilac," she added, "right now I'm going to appoint you Jill's monitor for next term."

The children clapped their hands and the

warm, pleased color spread through Lilac's face. Miss French put her arm around her.

On the last day they went home at noon.

" 'By, Miss French!" they called.

"Good-by, children, have a happy summer."

There were wild whoops as they burst from the school doors into the glorious, unbelievable summer freedom stretching endlessly ahead. Ellie did not whoop. Children who were taking pets home were climbing into cars beside their mothers. Ellie carried only an ivy plant. There seemed to be nothing to hurry home for.

As she turned into the yard, Pete was barking somewhere in back. Janie, whose class had been let out earlier, came tearing around the house. "Ellie!" Janie screamed. "Pete chased a baby squirrel into your garage! I saw it!"

"Let me see!" Ellie dumped her ivy on the step and followed Janie's flying heels. Pete, in the garage door, turned and barked his indignation. "Squirrel on our property!" Pete's bark said. There was no sign of the squirrel. Ellie brushed past Pete.

The garage held a clutter of garden tools, old window screens, and the children's stored or discarded toys. "Where is he?" Janie demanded, standing beside Ellie and looking around.

"Prob'ly hiding," Ellie said. She went over and moved her doll carriage, looking behind it. Next to it was Andy's express wagon, minus a wheel. Ellie pulled it out. Pete barked distractedly, poking his nose in wherever Ellie looked.

"Pete!" Ellie said finally. "You stop. I'm going to take you in the house." She took hold of his collar and led him firmly to the back door. "Now go on," she said. Pete went, his head hanging.

"Now we've got to look under everything," Ellie said, running back.

It was in the farthest, darkest corner that they found the squirrel at last. He was crouched, a tiny gray shadow, under an old cap of Andy's that someone had tossed there. Hunched together, cornered, he faced his pursuers with terrified eyes.

"Oh!" Janie said. "Get him, Ellie!"

Ellie knelt before the young squirrel. He tried to back closer against the wall. She put out her hand.

"He might bite or something," Janie cautioned.

"No," Ellie said, her eyes on the little creature. "You wouldn't, would you?" she asked him softly. Slowly, not to alarm him further, she touched his head, put out her other hand and gently gathered the tiny animal up.

"Oh, Janie," Ellie breathed, standing up and looking at the squirrel in her hands. "Feel how tiny he is! Why, there's hardly any of him inside the fluff!" The little squirrel fitted into one hand. "His heart's beating so hard!" Ellie said. "Don't be afraid," she told him soothingly. She held him firmly and carried him out of the garage just as Esther started down the back steps.

"Look at the baby squirrel, Esther!" Janie cried.

Esther stopped in her tracks and Ellie saw the quick, familiar look of alarm on her face. Ellie stood still, holding the squirrel against her with both hands, and faced her sister.

"He's afraid," she said, "but he doesn't bite or anything, Esther." The squirrel, its tiny heart racing against Ellie's hand, shrank close, trying to hide.

But Esther gave no cry of fear or alarm. She came slowly down the steps. "Where did you find him?" she asked, her eyes on the little squirrel.

Andy came home just then and had an explanation. "Some kids found a dead squirrel up the street," he said. "I bet that was its mother. Maybe this one fell out of the nest."

"Then he's an orphan," Ellie said. "But I'll take care of him." Her face fell and she glanced up at Esther. "Oh no! I can't keep him, can I?"

The screen door banged as Mister pushed his way out and came over to investigate. At sight of this new enemy the little squirrel struggled to get away, his eyes wild with terror.

"Oh!" Esther exclaimed suddenly. "He's scared!" She picked up the cat, dumped him inside the screen door, and came back. Then, to Ellie's utter astonishment, Esther reached out and gently touched the small gray head.

Ellie stared at her sister. "Esther!" she breathed. "You like him, don't you?"

Esther cautiously put out both hands and took the squirrel. Dumbfounded, Ellie let him go.

"Why, he's just a—a puff ball!" Esther held the soft, frightened thing gently, as Ellie had done. "I bet he's hungry," Esther said after a moment.

They tried peanuts. They tried crackers. The squirrel would not eat, but turned away and shrank against Esther. Her hand stroked his head. "Maybe he'd drink some milk," Ellie said finally, "like Jack and Jill." But the baby squirrel refused the milk they offered.

"He's just frightened to death," Esther said at last. "I'm going to take him in the house where it's quiet. Andy, let Pete and Mister out." She went up the steps, holding the little squirrel.

Ellie stared after her, her mouth open, then turned to Andy as he came back.

"I know what's eating her," Andy said softly, his eyes on the screen door that had closed after Esther. "People say, 'Are you the sister of the little girl who found the praying mantis nest? And do you like animals, too?' " Andy mimicked them. "She doesn't want anyone to know she's scared. So she's trying to like animals."

"She is?" Ellie gasped.

"You got to give her credit," Andy said, wandering off on business of his own.

Ellie stood still in the middle of the back yard, forgetting Janie, her thoughts in a whirl. Esther was trying to like animals! And the little, soft, helpless squirrel had won her heart.

All at once it seemed to Ellie that a dark cloud was dissolving into sunlight all around her. Through the cloud she had a glimpse of bright, wonderful summer stretching into the distance.

"Oh, Janie!" Ellie cried joyfully, clapping her hands and spinning around like a top.

"Ellie," Esther called, coming to the door still holding the squirrel, "come and help me fix a bed for him."

Ellie stopped spinning. She saw the house and the rosebushes whirl past her, but she was dizzier from happiness, it seemed to her, than from spinning around.

"Come on, Janie!" Ellie cried.

They made a bed of Esther's old brown sweater in a shoe box, put it in a dark corner of the basement, and gently set the little squirrel in it. Mister and Pete, both curious, were sternly excluded.

Later, when Ellie and Esther went down, the squirrel was not in his box. They hunted. No sign of him. That night he was still gone. "Oh!" Ellie moaned. "He got away."

"Maybe not," Daddy said. "He's probably hiding."

It was the next afternoon that Ellie stopped short part way down the stairs. From somewhere below came a small noise. She listened. There it was again—a chattering sort of sound. Ellie flew upstairs.

"Esther!" she called. "I think he's down there. Come quick."

Together they tiptoed down. The chattering stopped, then started. They hunted, following the sound. At last, in a dark corner behind a box of books, they found him. The little squirrel struggled weakly as Ellie took him up and put him in Esther's hands.

"Oh," Esther breathed, "poor baby!"

Ellie hung over him. "Maybe he'd drink milk now."

"Get some, Ellie."

Ellie flew for a saucer of milk. He would not lap, but Ellie dipped her finger in and held it to his mouth. Now at last the little squirrel licked, cautiously at first, then sniffed her finger hungrily, hunting for more. Ellie and Esther took turns dipping in their fingers.

"I think he's beginning to like us!" Ellie said joyfully.

The real reward came several days later. They had discovered that the little squirrel loved chocolate, and Ellie and Esther had each bought a chocolate bar with nuts for him. He sat up, took a piece of chocolate in both tiny paws and ate it daintily. Ellie and Esther knelt before him on the cellar floor.

The squirrel finished the chocolate, then, turning suddenly, leaped to Esther's knee, to her arm, and scrambled like a flash to her shoulder where he faced Ellie, sniffing for more candy.

Ellie, almost more startled than her sister, lost her balance. Esther's sudden alarm showed in her face, then faded quickly. Suddenly they both laughed delightedly. Esther eased herself into a better position. Ellie held out another scrap of chocolate and the squirrel's tiny claws closed trustingly around her fingers.

"He isn't one bit afraid now!" Esther said softly, looking down sidewise so as not to disturb him.

Ellie shook her head, holding more chocolate ready. "No," she said. Happiness sang in Ellie's voice. "And he likes us both just the same. So he's both of ours! Isn't he, Esther?"

Her cheek against the soft bit of fluff, Esther nodded at her little sister.

3718